CHURCH CHICK

MICHELLE CAREY

SUNRAI MULTIMEDIA

Church Chick

By Michelle S Carey

Published by Sunrai Multimedia

Copyright ©2011 Michelle S Carey

Cover Image: keeweeboy/bigstock.com & Sunrai Multimedia

Editing by: PWA, LLC

Dedicated to my loves - SeDona and Siyah

ABOUT THE AUTHOR

Born and raised in Washington, DC, Michelle developed a love for creative writing during her elementary school years. She discovered her passion for writing screenplays soon thereafter.

Michelle is a member of Zeta Phi Beta Sorority Inc. She currently resides in the Washington, DC area.

Connect with Michelle Carey

https://linktr.ee/michellecarey

1
---

*B*owie, Maryland

It was another boring Sunday, another Sunday of watching my mother suck up to the first family, another Sunday of listening to the Minister speak on what we should and should not do, and the last Sunday before the Saturday I was to get married.

Sabrina lay in her bed with the covers over her head. As her arm inched out from underneath, she fought to find the alarm clock and hit the snooze button. The clock continued to buzz as it fell to the floor near the stuffed animals. Sabrina poked her head out as the sun shone through her curtains.

Sabrina enjoyed laying in the bed for a minute or two while her thoughts drifted. She thought about her upcoming wedding and any last-minute details. The most important last minute detail was how she wanted to run away -- straight to the honeymoon -- without the groom. She smiled at the thought when her daydream was shattered from a knock on the door. I wish my mother wouldn't do that. That was Sabrina's cue; it was time to get up.

In her late twenties, Sabrina Sloan, still lived at home, and had the most beautiful almond-shaped brown eyes, smooth soft light brown skin and the darkest, longest black hair most had ever seen. But she hid her good looks behind ponytails and hair buns, loose dark-colored clothing and wearing little to no makeup.

Sabrina shuffled to the bathroom, with her eyes barely open she walked into a table in the hallway; crashing an old family photo to the floor breaking the glass into pieces. Sabrina was never short on having minor mishaps. As she picked up the frame and the glass, her younger sister Trisha, the glamorous, stylish hip and wild one, came from out of the bathroom dancing to the music from her iPod.

"Morning, sunshine!" Trisha yelled.

Sabrina gave Trisha half a wave. "Do you have to be so loud?"

"What?" Trisha yelled again and removed one earplug from her ear. "What did you say?"

By the time she's an old woman she's gonna be deaf! "You're yelling."

"No, I'm not." Trisha gave Sabrina the side eye.

Did she hear my thoughts?

Sabrina and Trisha always had a loving relationship. Sabrina was four years older than Trisha. During their younger years, Trisha didn't want to be anything like Sabrina. She watched how, their mother, Helen, made Sabrina strive for perfection and the pressure she was under to deliver, especially the older they became. Trisha was more of a daddy's girl in every way - rebellious, confrontational, and tactless. Trisha still loved Sabrina very much, but she always was more grounded and living life on her own terms - not Helen's.

Sabrina brushed off Trisha and cleaned up the mess on the floor. Sabrina tried to shoo Trisha away, but she wouldn't move; she continued to stand in the hallway watching her sister's every move.

Sabrina walked to the bathroom; the belt from her bathroom dragged on the floor. Trisha continued to look at her sister; as if she knew something funny would happen. Sabrina, a dragging belt, and glass were a lethal combination.

"If that girl didn't know any better, I would say she needed some serious help," Trisha said to herself.

As Sabrina closed the door, her belt was caught, and the only noises Trisha heard were a thud, the shattered glass hitting the floor once again, and Sabrina's moaning.

"Bingo!" Trisha laughed at her sister's misstep.

---

*H*elen Sloan in her early fifties, petite in stature, with reading glasses hanging around her neck, went to get the Sunday newspaper off the back porch for her husband Charles.

Helen had always been religious. Her father was heavily involved with the church. Her grandfather was a Deacon, and her great-grandfather was a pastor, when they lived in a small town in Virginia. Helen grew up in the country, were everyone knew everyone, and everyone's business. A small part of her always wanted to see to what the big city was like, just to see what the fuss was. Sometimes, she would sit on the hallway steps; eavesdropping on her mother, grandmother, and aunts talk about the latest gossip. The conversations were always centered on some woman being a whore, trying to steal their husbands.

Helen loved the church, and it was because of this love and her strong church principles that kept her stable and allowed her to be a good wife to Charles.

Charles Sloan, halfway dressed for church, entered the kitchen looking for her morning coffee and newspaper. Now in his early sixties, he was bald, and chunky around the mid-section.

Charles hadn't always been religious, not as much as Helen, but he believed in God. He was a good provider, husband, and father to his family, but church wasn't always high on list.

He never grew up in the church. His family only went to church on the last Sunday of the month; the Sunday the Pastor gave out food and money to the needy and his family stayed in need. When he met Helen, it was during a time; he knew his life needed to change. When he lived in Brooklyn, Bedford-Stuyvesant, as a young man, he got involved with the niece of a mafia underboss. Once word got around on the streets and back to her uncle she was fooling around with a Black man, Charles knew he wouldn't be able stay in Brooklyn. He took the first bus out of town when the underboss' soldiers came looking for him at his mother's house. He found himself in a small town in Virginia. He could find work in a warehouse where he worked with old man Henry Johnson, Helen's father, who introduced him to Helen at the annual company picnic. Facing death made him face God and Helen helped him. Helen never knew about his troubled past, and he kept it that way.

Charles always thought most of the things the Pastor said were rooted in common sense, and that he really didn't need a book to tell him he should not steal; he only went to church for Helen's sake.

As Helen returned from the back porch, she tossed the newspaper toward the table; she missed. The paper hit Charles in the face instead. He jumped and Helen didn't notice as if nothing had happened. She then fixed breakfast.

"Ms. Doris told me a sex doctor joined the church," Helen mentioned.

Charles ignored Helen and took a sip of his coffee when Sabrina stumbled into the kitchen.

Sabrina like her father wasn't dressed for church. She was dreading every second as the clocked ticked closer to ten thirty.

"Are you going to church today, Sabrina?" Charles asked, as he opened the paper and read the latest news about President Obama.

"Don't I always?" Sabrina said, with a hint of sarcasm.

Helen placed Sabrina's plate on the table and gave her a stern look - as if to say - never mess with the church and the Lord's work.

"Did you get my suit from U-Wongs?" Charles directed his attention back to Helen.

She knows I don't like watery eggs! Sabrina flicked the scrambled eggs and shook her head.

"I re-steamed your pants." Helen said, with a stone face.

"What's the point of redoing work the cleaners has done?" Sabrina asked.

Helen turned up her nose. "It wasn't crisp like Mr. Smith use to do them; they should have never sold that store to them foreigners! They're taking over everything. Got the Mexicans working in the McDonald's, A-rabs took over Seven Eleven, and the Koreans don't know how to fry chicken."

"Mother! You're so stereotypical and probably a borderline racist. Was that even necessary?" Sabrina asked.

"Now black people know how to fry chicken! What do Koreans know about frying chicken? Nothing! That's what I say!" Helen chuckled to herself.

Sabrina didn't like the fact her mother had problems with other cultures. On some days, Sabrina came close to calling her mother out on her ignorance, but today wasn't one those days. Today she wasn't up for the fight.

Helen ignored Sabrina and continued to rant about the cleaners and frying chicken when Trisha strutted into the kitchen dressed in a short red skirt and skintight white tank top.

"Oh no young lady, you're not wearing that to church!" Helen directed her words to Trisha without missing a beat.

"Why not? It's hot!" Trisha yelled back trying not to laugh at Helen.

"That's the problem. No child of mine, that's a child of God, is going anywhere looking like she's a spawn of Satan."

Charles continued to read his newspaper, ignoring the usual Sunday morning women chatter.

Sabrina chuckled. She loved to see her mother and sister go back and forth. It was always a battle of the wills. Sometimes Helen won, but most of the time Trisha won. Helen loved Trisha, even with her worldly ways. Trisha was the young woman Helen wanted to be.

"Whatever!" Trisha yelled back.

"It looks a little whorish," Sabrina nodded her head, agreeing with Helen.

"Maybe if you'd dressed a little more like a whore, you wouldn't be marrying that old man!" Trisha replied, trying to get under Sabrina's skin.

Forget you! Sabrina went into her feelings. "I don't need to listen to this!" She said, pouting.

Sabrina knew she shouldn't have tried to get in between them; she never had a rapid-fire response. At that point, she was tired of hearing about her wedding and Deacon Byrd.

"Charles, do you hear Trisha's foul mouth?" Helen asked.

Charles looked over his newspaper and watched his wife shaking the spatula at Trisha.

He heard her he's not deaf! Sabrina shoved the plate of watery eggs and burnt bacon away.

"Such a foul mouth child," Helen continued.

Sabrina knew this was her opportunity to exit, so she did.

"Sabrina, you've barely touched your breakfast," Helen said.

"It's because you really can't cook, Ma," Trisha added, getting that last little dig in, while making a bowl of cereal.

3

*S*abrina fumbled through her closet, looking at her dark and dreary clothes. She skimmed through a series of long black, gray, and blue skirts; tons of white shirts and blouses in two styles, high button up to the neck and long sleeve. In the back of her closet, hung a yellow sweater that longed to see the break of day. Sabrina couldn't remember how she got the sweater and why she didn't wear it more often.

As long as Sabrina could remember, she tried to be the good daughter her mother always wanted her to be. Being the oldest, Helen placed a lot of pressure on Sabrina to be perfect, to get the best grades, the most liked and never have her name associated with gossip with anyone at the church.

Sabrina selected a black skirt, white blouse, and pulled out the yellow sweater for good measure.

4

---

*N*ortheast, Washington, DC

Blair Brown, in her early thirties, a natural beauty, with olive skin, looked a lot like Jennifer Lopez. She never had to wear makeup, but her face had shown years of sadness in her hard life. Her father left her mother before she was born. Her mother, at the time her father left, didn't have a job, and didn't know how to support Blair. Eventually, Blair's mother became a prostitute and a drug addict.

By the time, Blair was five; she became a ward of the court and lived in and out of different foster homes. When she was sixteen, she was kicked out of her last foster home, when she was caught trying to seduce her foster father. From that point on, Blair was on her own. She eventually found work as a bartender. She landed her job at the Double Sky Bar and Lounge in the revitalized section of southwest DC when the owner of the last bar fired her for sleeping with her husband. She never knew what happened to her mother.

On her eighteenth birthday, she received a notice from the courts stating her mother had passed away before her fourteenth birthday. The courts couldn't disclose the information to minors. Included in the notice was a picture of her mother standing with a man. On the back of the picture, it read, '. S. and me', but at least one initial were faded.

Blair stared at a sleeping Tobin Peterson, in his early thirties, lying next to her. She ran her fingers down his muscular back. He twitched, and then she ran her fingers across his face. He batted her hand away as he woke up.

Tobin came to Washington, DC from Columbus Ohio. He was a musician looking to put together a jazz fusion band. His mother and father were good people and encouraged their children to challenge themselves. Tobin was the oldest of eight, an all-star athlete in high school, and graduated near the top of his class. He decided not to attend college, even though he had a full football scholarship to attend Ohio State. Instead, he decided to explore the music scene of different cities. Before he knew it, he had been moving from city to city for the last seven years but hadn't found a reason to settle down in anyone place.

Blair and Tobin lived together as roommates for a little over three months. Blair remembered the first day she saw Tobin. He answered the ad she put on Craigslist looking for a roommate. Blair had lost her job. She didn't know how she would pay her rent for her apartment, so she rented out her second bedroom. Tobin was the first person to inquire about the room, and she had a gut feeling to go with him. His Dwayne 'The Rock' Johnson good looks also helped. Tobin had been working two part time jobs during the day and playing different musical venues at night, but the gigs were sporadic.

"Good Sunday morning, handsome."

Tobin sat up and rubbed his light hazel eyes. He looked around the room trying to focus.

"Ah..." He said.

He jumped out of bed and grabbed his clothes from the floor as Blair rolled over to his side of the bed.

"Last night was wonderful! Thanks for hookin' a girl up!" Blair continued.

Blair stretched out in the bed and wrapped the sheet around her body; she felt exhilarated. She had been waiting for this moment for a while, but she didn't want to seem too anxious.

"I know we both swore. But — you know it goes." Blair gave him a smile.

Tobin turned to Blair and stared at her. He sighed.

"We're roommates Blair. We shouldn't have done this. We crossed the line." He put his underwear and pants on. He held on to his shirt continuing to expose his hairless chiseled muscular chest and six pack abs.

"Fall back for a sec; let's take a minute to think about this," Blair said.

"Think about what? We had drunken sex. That's it, nothing more to it."

Tobin wasn't in the mood to listen to any more of Blair's ramblings. He looked for his shoes and remembered he left them in the living room. The night before was foggy in his mind. He knew he couldn't make this mistake again. Blair liked him and all he wanted was ass. The ass wasn't even that great he concluded in his mind.

When Tobin reached for the door, Blair rose from the bed, while trying to keep the wrapped sheet around her body. She lunged at him and attempted to kiss him. He pulled back from her and pushed her away.

He left, slamming the door behind him.

5

*S*abrina walked behind her parents and sister as they entered the packed and busy church. Trisha winked at the young cute choir director as she filed into the church sanctuary. Once inside the church, Helen rushed over to the church matriarch, Mother Byrd and gave her a hug. Helen wanted everyone to know her family was close with the first family of the church. This would ensure her family was always cared for, and it gave her a sense of power.

As more people entered the church, Dr. Andrea Kent in her early forties walked in wearing the best Prada pants suit anyone in the church had ever seen; given the fact the majority of the elders didn't take kindly to women wearing pants to church or knew what Prada was. Dr. Kent looked as if she had stepped off the latest fashion runway, her makeup was flawless; her long dark-brown hair was flowing - not a strand out of place, and most of the men of the church could smell her sweet scent from a mile away. Dr. Kent was out of her element, but she didn't mind too much; the way she swayed her hips let everyone know in the church; she was confident and didn't care what people said or thought. Dr. Kent never had plans to be a long-term churchgoer; the chairman of the Deacon board, Wallace Byrd, invited her to his church one Sunday, and after that, she came at least twice a month.

Helen grabbed Charles' elbow. "That's her Charles, the one in the pants," Helen said, as other female elders of the church turned their heads in disgust as Dr. Kent sashayed by them.

Helen tried hard not to point at Dr. Kent, but Charles noticed the sway of Dr. Kent's hips over his glasses. He grinned a little while eyeing the back-and-forth motion of her hips and the way her ass bounced with each step, she took. Noticing her father's grin, Sabrina attempted to look over his shoulders to see what he was grinning about since Helen didn't notice. She noticed the bounce too. Trisha, never to be out done by anyone, walked past her family to catch up with Dr. Kent while pulling down her skirt.

"I told that child not to wear that mess!" Helen said, with embarrassment.

"Look at this way; at least she has on a skirt," Sabrina said, referring to Dr. Kent's pants suit.

Two female elders, Sister Smith and Sister Hardaway also got a hard look at Trisha walking behind Dr. Kent.

"Birds of a feather flock together," Sister Smith said.

"I know Sister Helen has tried her best with that girl but the devil just runs deep," Sister Hardaway said, shaking her head.

"We must continue to pray for Sister Helen."

As the two female elders take their seats, Cyrus Byrd, stopped Sabrina, a plain looking fellow, always had a crush on Sabrina, since as long as he could remember. Sabrina never paid any attention to Cyrus then and still didn't pay him any attention now.

"Sabrina?" Cyrus pulled Sabrina to the side behind a door leading to the upstairs pews, taking her hand.

"Cyrus, church is about to start and I need to be seated, so that..."

"So that Uncle Wallace can see you?"

Sabrina attempted to leave; and out of reaction, he grabbed her arm and jerked her around to face him.

"I think you're making a mistake." Cyrus' hands shook.

Sabrina yanked away from his grip. "Look! I have to go," Sabrina said, annoyed.

Sabrina left Cyrus standing there. He knew he shouldn't have approached her about marrying his Uncle Wallace, but he cared for her. They grew up together.

Deacon Wallace Byrd peered down at Sabrina when she took her seat close to the front pew. She was many years his junior, and it bothered him to see her mingling with Cyrus or other men her age. Not that he was jealous of them. At fifty, he was still a good-looking man, physically fit and showing no signs of aging. He took care of himself - hair dyed, nails polished and wore expensive clothes. Sabrina was perfect for him. She was nice-looking, but not too stunning to upstage him. However, he planned to keep an eye on Cyrus.

Soon after seeing Sabrina entering the sanctuary from the back door, Deacon Byrd witnessed Cyrus entering the sanctuary after her. What was going between his future wife and his nephew, he wondered. Even church members looked back at Cyrus with a disapproving eye.

Deacon Byrd scanned the rows of members sitting in the pews looking for Dr. Kent. He tried to contain his excitement when he saw her, he couldn't help himself, he couldn't hold it back; he gave her a quick smile before anyone could notice.

Dr. Kent was the woman Deacon Byrd always wanted, but his father, Minister Macon Byrd wouldn't approve. Dr. Kent was too worldly. It was bad enough she was coming to the church, but the Minister didn't know the Deacon invited her. Overall, Minister Byrd thought anyone was savable, including Dr. Kent, sexiness, and all.

Minister Byrd had no clue how or why Dr. Kent came to know

about his church, but whatever the reason he had his eye on her. Any woman commanding that kind of lustful attention deserved to be watched for any distrusting ways.

As the church service began, Sabrina looked at Minister Byrd, in his late seventies, shouting out to the congregation, as if they were all deaf. Minister Byrd was a short man, but he had a powerful voice. Sabrina always admired Minister Byrd, perhaps this why she agreed to marry his son; but father and son were nothing alike. Minister Byrd seemed to believe in what he preached to his core while his son seemed to enjoy the benefits of being a single Deacon and a minister's son. Most of the single women of the church practically threw themselves at his feet. When it was announced, the Deacon would marry Sabrina, most of the women thought it was because she was young and beautiful, and inexperienced. He could easily take advantage of her.

It was over a year ago, Minister Byrd told his son Wallace, he needed a beautiful young wife to help him carry on the legacy of the church. Sabrina has selected over many other women, mostly because of her multicultural looks.

"Love is in the air my people!" Minister Byrd shouted in his Barry White baritone voice.

Ms. Doris, a close family friend also in her seventies, sat next to Sabrina. Ms. Doris was the nosiest person in the church. She tried to get into everyone's business in the church. Helen always kept Ms. Doris close, not only to keep her out of her business, but also to find out about other people's business. She had always been like a grandmother to Sabrina and Trisha since their maternal grandmother died before they were born.

"Whew! It's hot in here," Ms. Doris said, as she fanned herself. "This sermon is for you child."

"As if, I didn't know," Sabrina thought.

Sabrina tuned Minister Byrd out. Instead, she focused on Dr. Kent. She noticed she was taking notes. She wondered what the good sex doctor was writing. Maybe it was how to help Deacon Byrd with a sexual dysfunction before the wedding night. Maybe it was to help Minister Byrd with getting it up. Sabrina didn't know; it could have been many possibilities, but whatever it was, it made her chuckle at the thought.

Caught in her thoughts, Deacon Byrd was not pleased with the look on Sabrina's face; he shot her a stern stare as he looked on from the pulpit.

"We're going to have love right here in our church next Saturday. Let the congregation say AMEN!" Minister Byrd continued to shout and pat the sweat from his brow.

"AMEN!" The congregation shouted back in unison.

Sabrina sunk low in the pew; she knew everyone could see the look he gave her while Dr. Kent flashed the Deacon a flirtatious smile. Deacon Byrd straightened up, but had to contain his excitement, as one of the elderly women caught wind of all the looks, she shook her head at Dr. Kent.

6

---

*A*fter Minister Byrd finished his sermon, most of the members of the church went to the basement. It was a well-known fact; the Church of God in Bowie, not only gave its community the best word of God, but also fed everyone the best Sunday dinner they ever had. Minister Byrd used the church's buffet style dinners to solicit more members, even going as far as advertising it in one of those low-budget commercials on television. Hear the word and be fed was his motto.

As members filed into the basement, long tables were already filled with people eating, and more members stood in the buffet line. The mood after Minister Byrd's sermon was always happy; parents didn't have to keep a close eye on their children and people could eat as much as they wanted. There was always enough food for many of the members to take home leftovers. Each Sunday was festive.

Elated by Sabrina's decision to marry Deacon Byrd, Helen liked to spy on the faces of the single women in the church who wanted to date the Deacon. Helen thought Sabrina was lucky. It made her smile every Sunday dinner to watch her daughter have the privilege to sit at the head table with the Byrd family, the first family of the church. Sabrina didn't feel any way about it. She hated sitting next to Deacon Byrd at the head table. Every Sunday, she looked around the room; she knew all eyes were on her, and it made her feel uncomfortable.

"We need to go pick up the license tomorrow morning. I will pick you up at 9am," Deacon Byrd said.

Ms. Doris fresh from the buffet line, with her plate piled high, sat next to Sabrina. Ms. Doris was never a thin woman. She had three husbands and seven children to prove men love a thick woman any day of the week.

"Wasn't any more seats, I'm sure the Byrds don't mind me taking a rest." She sighed as she caught her breath.

Before Ms. Doris could get a fork full of food into her mouth, Dr. Kent slid into a seat in front of Sabrina, Ms. Doris, and Deacon Byrd.

"Ladies, Deacon," Dr. Kent said.

"You can't sit here," Mr. Doris, blurted out, giving her an evil eye, even the devil would be proud.

"Ms. Doris, Dr. Kent is welcomed," Deacon Byrd said. "All God's children are welcomed." He smiled.

Ms. Doris turned away from everyone at the table.

Deacon Byrd gave Dr. Kent a nod and a smile. "Please stay." He offered.

"What time are you due at the church on Saturday?" Ms. Doris asked, changing the conversation and to let Dr. Kent know Deacon Byrd was engaged to Sabrina all in one question.

Sabrina glanced at Dr. Kent trying not to stare, but she found her beauty, style, and demeanor to be mesmerizing.

"Did you hear me Sabrina?" Ms. Doris continued.

"I think she hears you," Dr. Kent said.

Ms. Doris turned her chair more to Sabrina scraping it on the floor. "I wasn't speaking to you Miss High and Mighty."

Sabrina snapped out of her daze just before anyone could respond. "Please excuse me, I need air," she said, while leaving the table.

"No need for me to stay," Ms. Doris added.

"But you haven't finished your food Ms. Doris." Deacon Byrd noticed.

"The company you keep can make anyone lose their appetite." Ms. Doris grabbed her plate and left the table.

Dr. Kent unfazed by Ms. Doris' display of disapproval ate her piece of cake. Deacon Byrd watched Dr. Kent and imagined he was the cake.

7

_E_very Monday morning, Ms. Doris arrived at the church at dawn. She counted and then stacked the Sunday's offerings into piles. Ms. Doris liked to make the deposit when the bank opened just in case a church member tried to slip in a bad check. She always made sure the church received its money.

This Monday morning Sabrina arrived at the church earlier than normal. She was the church receptionist. It wasn't glamorous work, but she had a job and that was what mattered.

When she arrived, Ms. Doris was already sitting at the desk, counting Sunday's offerings, and placing the money into piles. One pile was for the Minister. The church paid all his bills, including his house. The remaining three piles were for the building fund; the Sunday buffet dinners and the Sunday offering which went for anything Minister Byrd chose, usually to help those members were in need.

The tiny office had two desks, with papers stacked everywhere. And heaps of newspapers piled high on top of the file cabinets. In the corner, sat at least thirty boxes filled with church records.

Sabrina could never figure out how the church functioned with so much junk in the office. However, Ms. Doris always made sure Minister Byrd's office was clean and inviting to all members.

Deacon Byrd entered the office; dressed clean and smelled good. Ms. Doris lit up like a Christmas tree when she saw him, "If I were twenty years younger, I'd go around that block any day of the week," she thought to herself.

"Sabrina, you ready?" He asked.

"For what?" she replied.

Sabrina knew it was the wrong answer. She could see the displeasure rise across his face.

Deacon Byrd eased over to Sabrina and pulled her close, so he could whisper in her ear. "Dammit! Didn't I tell you we had to go pick up the marriage license this morning!"

But Ms. Doris had hearing better than a dog. "Don't you remember child?" Ms. Doris asked.

Deacon Byrd checked himself in the mirror. He straightened his shirt and tightened his tie.

"I forgot."

'Damn, when we're married don't be wasting my time by forgetting shit. Hurry up! I got an appointment."

Ms. Doris excused Deacon Byrd's language; in her mind, he appeared stressed from the wedding. She knew even the best of men let out their frustrations.

Forget that. Sabrina tossed her wallet on the floor under her desk.

Deacon Byrd and Sabrina entered the Prince Georges County Courthouse. People lined the halls of the courthouse. They walked pass the busiest of the courtrooms - traffic and child support. Sabrina didn't know what to expect. She never had to go to court for anything in her life. Not even for a traffic ticket. Sabrina felt she like didn't belong, there was a certain element in the courthouse she had never encountered.

After walking up two flights of stairs and across the walkway connecting the new courthouse to the old, Deacon Byrd and Sabrina found the marriage license office.

"Good no one is here, we can get in and get out," Deacon Byrd said to Sabrina.

"Can I help you?" The clerk asked.

"We'd like to apply for a marriage license."

"I'll just need to see your identification and you need to fill out this form." The clerk pushed a clipboard with a form attached to it to the Deacon.

Sabrina was already sitting at the table next to the clerk's counter; Deacon Byrd sat across from her. He filled out the form and pushed it towards Sabrina for her to sign. She signed it.

Deacon Byrd called the clerk to come back over to the counter.

"May I see your identification please," she said.

Deacon Byrd took his ID out of his wallet. Sabrina searched her purse. She gave Deacon Byrd a look. He knew she didn't have her wallet. Sabrina didn't have to say a word.

"How in hell did you forget your wallet? Why would you even take it out of your purse," he ranted on with a raised voice.

"I must have dropped it," Sabrina said, "It's probably back at the church office."

"This will set us back," he said, "I'll call Ms. Doris have her look for it. You will repay her, somehow, if she finds it."

Sabrina walked over to the window; she snickered at the thought of how pissed he was.

"Don't worry about it," the clerk stated. "We only need the ID of either the bride or the groom."

Deacon Byrd could still apply for the license, even after all his ranting and complaining.

Fudge, but it was still fun to watch him get upset, all for nothing. Sabrina snickered again.

8

*D*owntown Washington, DC - Connecticut Avenue and
K Street

The buzzer sounded on Dr. Kent's phone. She paused for a
moment before answering.

"Yes, thank you. Send him in. No interruptions please," Dr.
Kent said, to her receptionist.

Andrea Kent had come a long way from Georgia. To have an
office on the prestigious Connecticut Avenue in Washington, DC,
wasn't easy. Dr. Kent worked her way through undergraduate and
medical school. She believed in herself, and her good looks
helped put her on top. And she liked being on top in all situations.
Being a therapist had its downs and ups, but she enjoyed the crazi-
ness of it all.

She took a pocket mirror from out of her purse, touched up
her flawless makeup and a lint brush from the desk drawer; she
brushed any lint balls from her suit jacket; then sprayed perfume
on her wrists and behind her ears. She struck a seductive pose on
her desk when there was a light knock on the door.

"Enter," she said.

Deacon Byrd entered the office. He rubbed his hands together as Dr. Kent continued to hold her pose on the side of the desk. Exquisite, he thought to himself. He ever had anyone as beautiful and as accomplished as her, even his first wife wasn't as fashionable as Andrea was. He married his first wife before he was twenty-two, only because his father thought it was better than him sleeping around with many women, making the church look bad. This was Minister Byrd's way of keeping his son clean.

He grabbed Dr. Kent.

"Damn, what kind of perfume are you wearing?" He asked; and kissed her on the neck. "It's driving me crazy."

Dr. Kent let her head roll back as he sniffed her perfume behind her ear. She loved when he sniffed behind her ear. Dr. Kent enjoyed Deacon Byrd's company. She wasn't interested in having a relationship or joining his church and being a part of the first family, she was only interested in having sex with him when she could. He had told her many times before he would give up Sabrina if she gave him the chance.

Deacon Byrd cared for Sabrina. He wasn't in love with her. The only reason he was marrying her was because his father thought she looked like the perfect minister's wife. Minister Byrd planned to let Wallace take the reins of the church next year when he retired. And Dr. Kent didn't have the heart of the church members like Sabrina. Everyone knew Sabrina would make a sincere and compassionate first lady of the church.

Deacon Byrd was willing to throw his hopes of being the next minister of the Church of God away for Dr. Kent. He wanted to be with her that much.

"Wow, you're good as this," she said, in a low whisper. He kissed her with passion. His blood rushed through his body, straight to his penis. He was ready to give her all his good loving.

Deacon Byrd moved his hands up the inside of Dr. Kent's skirt. He made his way to her sweet spot.

She moaned as he pulled her skirt up and attempted to pull her underwear down, but she stopped him. Deacon Byrd loved how she looked in her red garter belt and stockings, much sexier then pantyhose.

He slid off her suit jacket and unbuttoned her blouse exposing her lace bra. He unsnapped it from the front exposing her perky breasts. Dr. Kent never had much in the way of breasts but made up for it in the ass department. He sucked her nipples. He worked his way down her body. In the heat of the moment, Dr. Kent pushed some of the items on her desk to the floor; she needed more space to get into a better position. With her skirt up to her hips, Deacon Byrd pulled Dr. Kent's underwear to the side. Before she could get in a comfortable position, Deacon Byrd tasted her sweet spot. She grabbed him by the head and let him go to work.

9

Sabrina lay across the bed and stared at her wedding dress hanging on the door, a beautiful dress with a long satin train and lace sleeves. To her, the dress represented, a sweet and pure woman, marrying the man she loved; far from where she thought, she was with the Deacon. As Sabrina got lost in her thoughts, Trisha entered her room.

Trisha placed a box of nail polish on the bed before she hopped on the bed with her sister. They lay next to one another, and they both stared at the dress.

"Are you ready?" Trisha asked.

"I'm scared; I don't know what to expect or what he expects."

"You can always walk away."

"Can I? I made this promise. I can't back out now."

"Why do you think he's marrying you?"

"Older men fear death; I help him feel young again; I suppose."

Trisha slid off the edge of the bed and fell to the floor. She grabbed the box of nail polish she placed on the bed. She looked through the various colors; picked one and painted her toenails.

"Deacon Byrd, of all people, why him?" Trisha shook her head.

"He reminds me of Daddy."

"Stale?"

Sabrina laughed. Trisha always had a good sense of humor, even if the humor was embedded in the truth.

"More like solid." Sabrina continued.

"I know what I like solid, and it ain't Deacon Byrd!" Trisha shouted.

Both Sabrina and Trisha laughed at the thought of Deacon Byrd having a limp dick. They smiled at one another. The thought of Deacon Byrd wanting to have sex with Sabrina made her wince. Sabrina had fear written all over her face, she threw a pillow at Trisha hoping she wouldn't notice her anxiety.

The week went by too fast for Sabrina. The rain poured hard as the wedding guests arrived at the church. In one of the church basement's backrooms, there were people running around helping the bridesmaids. Some bridesmaids got their makeup done; others got the finishing touches done to their hair.

Helen and Ms. Doris helped Sabrina into her dress. Once Sabrina's dress was on, Helen and Ms. Doris admired her.

"My God child you look so special. This is a good choice for you, marrying Deacon Byrd." Ms. Doris said, reassuring Sabrina.

"I was thinking you'd never get married, but God has made a way," Helen added.

Helen clapped her hands once as she marveled at Sabrina's beauty. She always knew Sabrina would make a lovely bride.

Sabrina looked at herself in the mirror. She turned away from Helen and Ms. Doris. Her hands became sweaty, and her head began to hurt. If she could only get through the next twenty-four hours — the wedding and the wedding night — she knew she would be okay.

"I knew a man would want a good girl like you."

"I knew it, too. Sabrina is such a good girl. It's that other child of mine I worry about," Helen said.

Close by was Trisha; she sat in a chair spinning around. "No need to worry about me." Trisha continued to swirl around. "I'm just fine."

"Trisha, stop spinning in that chair before you get sick or mess up your hair," Helen said.

Trisha kept spinning in the chair when there was a loud knock on the door. "It's time!" The man said, on the other side of the closed door.

The bridesmaids hurried out the basement backroom. Helen looked at Sabrina a second time.

"It's time," Helen said, "This is so exciting."

Trisha spun around in the chair for the last time before getting up. "Yep, sure is, now let's get this freak show on the road." Helen gave Trisha a dirty look while pushing her out the door.

"Sometimes, I can't believe you're my child." Helen said and shook her head. If Trisha's hair were not done, Helen would have had enough nerve to hit her over the head.

Trisha laughed at her mother. "Ooooh, I'm so scared," Trisha said sarcastically.

"Well, are you coming child? It's your day," Ms. Doris said, walking to the door.

Sabrina remained behind. She stared at herself in the mirror. Her wedding dress fit her perfectly. The train was long; longer than any train she had ever seen. The aroma of her beautiful bouquet smelled as if she was in a field of fresh roses.

She didn't want to leave the room. She always wanted to be married, but not like this. Everything happened so fast, like how she got engaged, it was almost like a brokered deal between two companies. But Sabrina was too scared to back out of the merger for fear of retribution.

"If only I could have loved like I've never experienced," she whispered. Sabrina closed the door as she exited the church basement backroom.

~

The music played throughout the sanctuary. This was the biggest event the church had seen in years. Everyone was excited and ready to witness Miss Sabrina Sloan marry old man Deacon Wallace Byrd.

The wedding coordinator closed the doors, she glanced over each bridesmaid before the door was opened to allow them to walk down the aisle.

Each bridesmaid and the flower girls walked down the aisle while Charles waited with Sabrina out of sight from the wedding guests. He smiled at Sabrina and patted her hand, sensing Sabrina's anxiety. Her hands were sweaty and cold. He wasn't sure what do, should he stop the wedding and find out what was wrong? Or should he have chalked it up to nerves and let things be, he decided on the latter. This was Sabrina's day. He didn't want to ruin it for her, with all his speculations.

The wedding coordinator closed the doors again after the ring bearer was ushered down the aisle between the two junior bridesmaids. She fixed Sabrina's veil, picked any lint off of Charles' tuxedo jacket, and straightened out Sabrina's train. Perfect.

The organist played Here Comes the Bride. The doors opened. Revealed to the full packed church, everyone sighed in unison. Sabrina was stunning. With her arm wrapped around her father's, they began the journey to the altar. For Sabrina, it seemed like the end of the aisle was miles away and was closing like a dark tunnel. No matter how fast Sabrina wanted to run away, the end of the aisle kept getting closer. If only Sabrina could ditch this feeling of wanting to run in the opposite direction. If only Deacon Byrd didn't look scary as he stood at the end of the dark tunnel with a goofy lustful face. If only her father could feel her pain and call it off.

By the time Sabrina reached the end of the aisle, she felt a piercing pain in her head. Charles placed Sabrina's hand into Deacon's Byrd's; Sabrina knew she had to get it together.

"Your hands are soaked, Sabrina," Deacon Byrd said.

Sabrina tried to pull her hand back. He pulled her closer.

"No need to fear anything," He smiled at Sabrina. All she could see were his huge white horse teeth. She inched away, sensing her hesitation; Deacon Byrd grabbed her hand tighter.

This is crazy. Sabrina mustered up a fake smile. What am I doing here? How the hell did I get myself in this situation?

Sabrina was never a big proponent on swearing, but she felt the need to exercise independence, if only in her mind.

Excuse me Lord. Sabrina and Deacon Byrd stood before Minister Byrd.

Two of the elder churchwomen noticed a small struggle between Sabrina and Deacon Byrd as he tried to keep Sabrina close.

"If there is anyone who wishes to object to this union, please give us a sign," Minister Byrd said.

SOMEONE GIVE A GOT DAMN SIGN! Sabrina's hands became sweatier, and she felt uncomfortable in her wedding dress. The church was spinning.

I can't get sick, not now, be calm. Sabrina took a deep breath.

The back door slammed.

"Thank God!" Sabrina whispered.

The entire church turned to look at the back door. Cyrus eased into the back of the sanctuary.

Damn of all people to save me. Sabrina looked at Cyrus. Well, it's better than nothing, just say the words Cyrus.

"Cyrus, do you object to this union?" Minister Byrd asked.

Cyrus paused. It was the longest pause Sabrina had ever experienced in her life.

"No, no I don't," Cyrus said. Even though he wanted to call it off, for the sake of his own feelings, but he didn't know how Sabrina would feel about it.

Sabrina stood at the altar with what felt like millions of little beady eyes staring at her back; she waited patiently. She felt doomed. Damn you Cyrus.

"Family and friends...welcome...we are gathered here today for the union of Miss Sabrina Sloan and Deacon Wallace Byrd." Minister Byrd continued.

Sabrina turned to face Cyrus; she cut him the meanest look.

Inner Harbor, Baltimore, Maryland

Sabrina felt overwhelmed at what was to come during the wedding night. She made it through the wedding. Now, she knew Deacon Byrd would want ass, and she wasn't interested in giving him any.

As Sabrina and Deacon Byrd arrived at the hotel, Sabrina tripped and fell getting out of the car. Seeing this, didn't please the Deacon. He kneeled over Sabrina.

"Don't embarrass me, shit." Deacon Byrd rose; he straightened his tie and walked into the hotel. The valet helped Sabrina up.

Deacon Byrd approached the hotel clerk standing behind the registration desk.

"Welcome to the Hyatt. How may I help you?"

"I reserved a suite." Deacon Byrd said.

Sabrina wasn't surprised they only went to the Hyatt in downtown Baltimore. Deacon Byrd made it appear, they were going somewhere nice, like New York City, but she knew they were not getting on a plane, train, or a bus, so it had to be within driving distance. Sabrina knew Deacon Byrd was cheap; she didn't think he was this cheap. At the wedding, he promptly had Ms. Doris secure the monetary gifts. Sabrina wasn't aware of how much money was collected. She didn't care; he could have it all.

As Sabrina walked into the lobby of the hotel, she saw Dr. Kent walking from the hotel bar. She wasn't sure if this was a coincidence or if the Deacon invited her to their honeymoon.

Is he into threesomes? For a moment, Sabrina, and Dr. Kent's locked eyes on one another. To break Sabrina's stare, Dr. Kent winked at her. Sabrina didn't know if that meant something; was she supposed to wink back? Sabrina looked over at Deacon Byrd at the registration desk; he didn't notice Dr. Kent.

Once they found their honeymoon suite, Sabrina was still filled with anxiety from going through with the wedding and the fact the honeymoon was nowhere but at the downtown Hyatt - in of all places, Baltimore. The whole affair wasn't romantic. This is what my life has come too.

"You don't mind if I don't carry you over the threshold, I have a bad back."

"No I don't mind," Sabrina walked into the room.

"Excuse me for a minute, I need to go to the bathroom," Deacon Byrd said.

Sabrina went to look out the window at the beautifully lit skyline while Deacon Byrd rushed to the bathroom. Sabrina wondered what the world offered. She thought back on her life. She went to college. She received her Associates degree from the community college; but she never thought about finishing school to receive her Bachelors. She never felt stuck. She knew her parents would let her live with them forever, and Minister Byrd would let her work at the church as long as she wanted.

Sabrina's thoughts were broken as Deacon Byrd emerged from the bathroom. She waved her hands back and forth from the horrible smell. This can't be happening. What have I gotten myself into? I don't want to live with that smell for the rest of my life.

Deacon Byrd hunched over.

"Whew! Those beans Ms. Doris fixed must have settled in my lower half."

"Can you please shut the bathroom door?" Sabrina asked, "Consideration please."

"Girl, we are married. There are no considerations." Deacon Byrd patted the bed. "Come sit down."

"Um, I think we should talk first," Sabrina said.

"Imma give you something to talk about!" Deacon Byrd lunged for Sabrina. "UH!" He screamed.

Deacon Byrd clutched his chest. "Damn, what did that woman put in them beans?"

"I hope it wasn't some Viagra," Sabrina said, "You shouldn't have eaten so many. That's my wifely advice to you." Sabrina stepped back from him.

"This is no time for any jokes!" He shot back at her, "I'm not feeling well."

Deacon Byrd stumbled to the floor, grabbing the bed, and pulling the bed spread with him.

THUD! Deacon Byrd hit the floor like a knocked out heavy-weight fighter.

Sabrina looked at him on the floor. He didn't move. She approached him and tapped him with her foot, he still didn't move. She rushed to the phone.

10

*S*outhwest, Washington, DC

The Double Sky Bar and Lounge was crowded when Tobin arrived. The strobe lights bounced off the mirrors creating an illusion of diamond sparkles on the walls. The dance floor vibrated with the movement of the young hip professionals as the DJ spun all the best records from the booth up above. There was a flurry of activity between the waiters serving drinks and food, trying not to get caught dancing to the music. Tobin searched for a seat at the bar.

Blair spotted Tobin. "Hey, boo!" She yelled at him over the loud music.

She grabbed a beer glass and poured him a beer, then pushed it his way.

"We need to talk!" He yelled back at her.

Blair made a motion for Tobin to drink.

Tobin took a sip of the beer and looked around at the crowd in the bar. He even tried to scope out some of the single women, but he knew with Blair around he wasn't going to get very far.

"Drink up! We can talk later!" She shouted, while giving him a sweet smile and a wink.

Hours later, Tobin lay sound asleep in Blair's bed, with her next to him. She looked at the clock; the time read 6:30am. She pulled out a little silver box from her nightstand top drawer. She searched inside the case and took out a joint; and rummaged around for a match. Annoyed she didn't find one; she took a sip of her beer instead while flipping through the channels on television.

Tobin flinched as Blair rubbed her leg onto his. He slowly awoke.

"What time is it?" He asked, rubbing his eyes.

"It's still early yet. It's about 6:30."

Tobin gazed at his surroundings; he lay in the bed for a minute and stared at the ceiling. His head ached from drinking too much again. He had lost control of his senses and what he was doing. Now he had to make his move and get out of her room without causing a scene.

Blair scooted closer to him. She tried to snuggle under this arm when he leaped out of the bed.

"I gotta go. I got a gig to prepare for," Tobin said, while putting his pants on.

Blair sighed. "This is straight bullshit boo!" She yelled at him as her eyes widened. Blair didn't like how Tobin never wanted to stay around after they had sex.

"Hol' up! Who the fuck are YOU yelling at?" Tobin huffed.

Blair got up out of bed and looked for her clothes. She put her jeans and her shirt on and approached Tobin. She stood only inches from his face.

"It wasn't some straight bullshit when you were diggin' up in me last night!" Blair continued full throttle. "Damn you can't spend no time witcha girl?"

Tobin took a step back from Blair. "Nah."

"I don't know what the fuck you think this is, but you're not going to keep fucking me and then giving me hell about it in the morning." Blair stood firm in Tobin's face.

"You're crazy. You get me drunk, seduce me, but I'm the one giving you hell! Get the fuck outta here!"

Tobin finished putting his clothes on. The last thing he needed was to catch a domestic violence case with his crazy roommate.

"I'm outta this bitch!" He left.

Blair stood alone in the room. "Niggas, I swear!"

11

*M*ount Oak Cemetery, Woodmore Maryland

As on her wedding day, the rain poured. Sabrina glanced at all the people who came out to the cemetery to lay Deacon Byrd to rest. She didn't know he was liked by so many people.

Sabrina sat next to a visibly shaken Minister Byrd, his only son, dead from a heart attack. Deacon Byrd never liked to go to the doctor. Even though he had nicely defined muscles, he didn't like to do cardiovascular exercises, and he never liked to eat right. He lifted weights often, but he had an undetected block artery, a plaque buildup.

No one in the church expected Deacon Byrd would die on his wedding night; whispers around the church where that Deacon Byrd died on top of Sabrina while consummating their marriage. But she knew the truth; consummation didn't happen. Sabrina wanted to get the marriage annulled, despite Deacon Byrd being deceased. She wanted to pretend none of it ever happened.

As Deacon Byrd's casket was lowered into the ground, the rain continued to fall; a crack in the clouds opened; the sun peered through; and a small rainbow appeared. Sabrina knew better things were to come.

The Sloans and the Byrds made their way back to the church for the repast. While they rode in the limo, Minister Byrd turned to Sabrina.

"Sabrina, what were my son's last words?"

Unsure if she should tell the Minister the truth, his son was mad because he thought Sabrina made a joke about him needing Viagra, falling, and eating the beans, didn't sound right.

"Minister Byrd, no words; he fell to the floor, without warning." That was the best thing she could say.

The Byrds and the Sloans arrived at the church; and were ushered into the church basement, Sabrina needed to speak to Rachel, Deacon's Byrd's daughter, but she disappeared. The church basement decorated in Deacon Byrd's favorite colors, purple and black, for the Baltimore Ravens, made tears fall from Minister Byrd's eyes. The female church elders surrounded Minister Byrd to comfort him. The last member of the Byrd family to pass was his wife. She died of cancer fifteen years prior.

Mourners ate their dinner, trying to get a glimpse of Sabrina sitting at the head table. Sabrina sat next to Minister Byrd as church members comforted him as he wept. No one comforted Sabrina.

The thought of all the sadness in the room gave Sabrina a headache. She needed to leave. Grabbing an umbrella from under the table, she slipped out of the church basement unnoticed, except by Dr. Kent.

Outside, the sun shone bright. Sabrina tilted her head to let her skin soak up the warm rays. She rocked her head back and forth, as Dr. Kent approached her from behind, and tapped her on the shoulder, BAM! Sabrina swung out with the umbrella.

Stunned, Dr. Kent almost fell from the force of the hit. "WOW!" Dr. Kent wailed.

"I'm so sorry."

"Are you always this much on the defense?" Dr. Kent rubbed her arm.

"No. I'm just tired."

Dr. Kent pulled a business card from her Gucci purse and handed it to Sabrina.

"Make an appointment; you seem like you need it."

Sabrina didn't budge as Dr. Kent tried to hand her the business card.

"No thank you. I don't need your kind."

"My kind? What does that mean? I don't see what Wallace saw in you."

"I don't have any 'special' issues," Sabrina said as she looked around and took a few steps away from Dr. Kent. "Plus, what didn't Wallace see in me?" Sabrina's eyebrow rose. Was Deacon Byrd seeking help from the good doctor?

Dr. Kent took Sabrina's hand and placed the card in her palm, ignoring Sabrina's question.

"Why don't you hold on to that - just in case? I see adventure in your eyes."

Sabrina stared at Dr. Kent as she walked to her car. Standing on the steps, holding the business card, confused about the interaction she had, she admired how Dr. Kent walked and spoke; she was sexy and confident; the things she lacked

That woman is so mysterious. Wanting to follow her and probe her more, on what she meant, Sabrina let it go...for now. It wasn't the right time.

After Dr. Kent walked out of sight; Sabrina read the business card, tucked in her bra, and went back into the church.

Upper Marlboro, Maryland

Sabrina searched for a parking space near Deacon Byrd's house on the corner. An unusual number of cars parked close to the house, and she noticed people sitting on the well-manicured lawn. Sabrina parked a distance away; she didn't know what to expect from her stepdaughter, Rachel. Deacon Byrd and Rachel didn't have the best relationships, but Sabrina wanted to believe the Deacon loved Rachel in his own way.

The closer Sabrina got to the house; she heard the loud music coming from the house. When Sabrina entered the house, guests danced in what used to be the living room, and the smell of marijuana and alcohol lingered in the air. Drunk and high young adults crawled every inch of Deacon Byrd's house.

What the hell is going on here? Sabrina coughed as she entered the main dining room; what replaced the antique dining room table were four card tables. The partygoers played Dominos, Spades, Strip Poker, and the last table was dedicated to joint sales.

Sabrina went to the kitchen; Rachel, Deacon Byrd's daughter, approached her.

"What's going on here?" Sabrina asked.

Rachel's eyes were like glass.

"What does it look like, Mary Poppins?" Rachel slurred. "It's a party."

"Well, isn't that supercalifragilisticexpialidocious," Sabrina shot back.

"Supercally what?" Rachel grabbed her mouth.

"This is unacceptable. Your father wouldn't approve of this."

"My father is dead!" Then, Rachel threw up on the floor near Sabrina's shoes. "Plus, he never cared!"

Sabrina was lucky Rachel missed her mark. She waited for Rachel to get herself together. Rachel wiped her face with the bottom of shirt.

"I'm going to call the cops." Sabrina pulled out her cell phone, walking out of the hallway towards the stairs.

"You were only married to my old man for - what - five maybe six hours at the most; that's not enough time for you to act like you wanna play mommy!"

"I live here now."

"No, the fuck you don't!"

Rachel was becoming belligerent the more they spoke. But Sabrina didn't know where else to go. She had already moved her things out of her parent's house, shortly before the wedding. She had been staying at a hotel; the week after Deacon Byrd passed. Sabrina had been trying to catch up with Rachel all week. Deacon Byrd hadn't given her the keys, yet.

Sabrina moved pass Rachel to get up the stairs. Rachel stuck her foot in front of Sabrina and blocked her. Sabrina tripped on the first stair.

"I've already moved my things in."

"So, you can move your things out." Rachel opened the hall closet door enough for Sabrina to see the boxes. "I have your stuff right here in this closet, no need for you to go any further."

Sabrina peeked at the stacked boxes; then dismissed Rachel.

"I'll be back in the morning." Sabrina walked out of the house.

"I bet you will." Rachel slammed the door shut.

Sabrina shook her head as she walked away from the house and made a disturbing the peace call to the police.

After that, Sabrina didn't deal with Rachel anymore. She didn't want Deacon's Byrd house anyway.

Lake Waterford Park, Pasadena Maryland

Another couple of weeks had passed, and the trees were blooming. It was the newest and freshness of spring. Kids played on the playground; joggers jogged around the two-mile wide lake, while other people sailed their miniature portable motorized boats.

Helen and Sabrina strolled around the lake; Sabrina noticed a poster pinned to a tree about a speed-dating event. She caught Dr. Kent's name on the flyer.

"Sabrina, I am worried about you," Helen said.

"I am fine."

"You are such a young woman, having to experience something so awful."

Maybe it wasn't so awful; I really didn't love him.

Two kids run across their path on their way to the playground, almost running into them.

"Maybe it wasn't so awful," Sabrina slipped.

Sabrina picked up a rock and threw it into the lake. The rock almost hit a miniature portable motorized boat. A man screamed at her from afar. Behind her mother's back, Sabrina gave the man the finger. The motion shocked her. She did it so quickly; she didn't know what to think. Did I do that?

"Sabrina, what are you saying?"

"Oh, mother. What I meant was...maybe I asked for it."

"You need to repent. This is blasphemy! You didn't pray for your husband to die. Did you?"

Helen's words were inaudible too Sabrina, as she continued to walk.

I'm sure Deacon Byrd was a nice man, in his own little way, but for one, he was too old for me and two I'm glad he's gone. Minister Byrd would have never allowed a divorce. His first wife had to get out by death!

"Did you?" Helen asked again.

Sabrina gazed at the lake.

"Do you hear me talking to you?"

Sabrina stayed in her own thoughts.

⁓

Blair entered her apartment. The phone rang. She hopped over the sofa to answer the phone.

"Hello." Blair paused. "Tobin?"

She held the line for a brief ten seconds before the phone went dead.

Blair shuffled into Tobin's room; he wasn't there. She picked his pants up off the floor and searched through his pockets. She found a balled-up cocktail napkin from Mookie's Jazz Club with a woman's name and phone number. She kicked the bed.

12

———

*S*abrina arrived at the church office. Papers, everywhere, she attempted to clean up the mess in the office. She filed papers into folders. Ms. Doris arrived thirty minutes after she did.

"What are you doing here?" Ms. Doris patted Sabrina on the back.

"Working." Sabrina moved one-step over, so Mr. Doris wouldn't continue to touch her.

Why else would I be here?

Cyrus entered the office.

"You should rest, child." Ms. Doris moved papers off of her desk.

Sabrina slammed the papers on the desk. Ms. Doris and Cyrus were startled by the noise.

"Ms. Doris, I think you are right. I quit." Sabrina gathered her things and left.

Damn, that was easy, like pressing an easy button. Sabrina singed in her head. Walk on by...

"Wow," Cyrus said.

"Is she serious? I didn't tell her to quit!" Ms. Doris miffed.

"I think she's serious." Cyrus looked around the room, seeing that Sabrina was gone.

"Who's gonna answer the phone?" Ms. Doris asked, with a grimaced face.

Cyrus shrugged his shoulders. "Not I!" He waved bye and left.

The phone rang. Ms. Doris frowned at the phone. "Ugh!"

Sabrina entered her parent's house. Helen came from the living room into the front hallway with her hair messy and her clothes half off, attempting to fix her hair and clothes.

"Sabrina! What are you doing home so early?"

Charles came from the living room with his pants unzipped but buttoned and his shirt sticking through the zipper hole.

"I thought you were at work!"

Sabrina not surprised her parents still had sex; was surprised they didn't always stick to the bedroom.

"Surprised to see me?"

Sabrina nodded her head to her father. He looked down at his pants and turned around.

"I quit my job." Sabrina ran up the stairs to her bedroom.

"Charles, the child is insane!"

Helen clutched Charles' arm and widened her eyes, looking for answers from him. Charles shrugged his shoulders.

"Well, don't look at me! I have no idea what's going on."

Helen went to the stairs as the phone rang. The caller ID read: CHURCH OF GOD.

"First her husband, now her job," Helen said, "What's next?"

Charles answered it. "It is Ms. Doris."

Instead of going upstairs, Helen stood close to Charles trying to listen in on the conversation.

"Well, is that right?"

Charles covered the phone. "Sabrina quit her job," he said to Helen.

"That's what Sabrina said." Helen pointed out to Charles.

～

Sabrina rummaged through the packed boxes in her room. She heard the commotion downstairs but continued to toss things out the boxes left and right. She stood in the room, searched through the clothes and items on the floor again. She examined the mess. She searched one last box before she gave up. She left her room.

～

Charles continued to listen to Ms. Doris on the phone. Sabrina trotted down the stairs.

"Ms. Doris is on the line right now young lady!" Helen shouted.

Sabrina walked out the house. The door slammed before Helen could say another word.

～

Sabrina arrived back at the office. Ms. Doris still seated at the desk in front of the money piles, missed her Monday morning deposit.

"I knew you'd come to your senses." Ms. Doris wrote out the deposit slip and prepared to go to the bank. "Did your parents have a talk with you?"

Sabrina didn't hear Ms. Doris. She continued her search mission.

"Excuse me; I need to get inside the desk drawer."

Ms. Doris moved out of Sabrina's way; Sabrina shifted through the stuff in the desk. She reached far into the drawer. She found Dr. Kent's business card.

"This is all I needed." Sabrina left.

"Helen was right; the child has gone mad!" Ms. Doris said and plopped back into the chair.

The phone rang; she threw her hands into the air. "I'm never going to get to the bank!"

Sabrina sat in front of the church and called Dr. Kent's office on her cell phone. She made an appointment.

Sabrina, Trisha, Helen, and Charles sat at the dining room table. The bowls of food passed back and forth to one another as they put food on their plates. The most sound anyone heard was the scraping of folks against the plates.

"Can someone speak please?" Trisha asked.

"Trisha, please! Now is not the time," Helen said.

"Enough is enough!" Trisha shot back at Helen.

Sabrina continued to sit in silence. She watched her mother, and sister go back and forth.

"Everybody calm down," Charles said.

"So what Sabrina quit her little church job." Trisha continued. "People change jobs every day."

Sabrina flicked her food around on her plate.

"Sabrina, do you have anything you want to say for yourself?" Charles asked.

"Yes."

Helen stared at Sabrina; she waited for her answer.

"I'm going to bed." And with that, Sabrina left.

Helen put her hands together to pray, "What more as mother do I have to do?"

"Learn to cook better could be one," Trisha answered Helen in a God like booming voice.

"I've had enough of you, young lady," Charles said to Trisha.

"Never heard from a man before," Trisha blew a kiss to Charles.

The lights were dim in Charles and Helen's room. Helen got in the bed next to Charles. He continued to read his magazine.

"Something is wrong with Sabrina," Helen said.

"Sabrina is fine, Helen."

"I think the devil's got her mind. I think she prayed for the Deacon to die."

Charles continued to read, "Sabrina did no such thing, and she has been through a lot these last few weeks. Give her a break Helen."

"She needs to apologize to Ms. Doris tomorrow, first thing in the morning," Helen mentioned.

"Go to sleep, before I pray, he'll put you to sleep," Charles said annoyed. He dropped the magazine on the floor; placed his glasses on the night table and turned off the light, "We'll deal with this in the morning, okay?"

Helen sighed.

_____

13

*T*obin entered the apartment. Blair slinked out to the living room from her bedroom.

"Where the hell have you been?" Blair yelled, as she paced the floor blocking him from moving.

"What?" Tobin asked, as he dodged her.

"Your ass hasn't been home in days."

"Come home? I'm an ass-grown man! I don't owe you anything."

"Dang, boo I was just askin'."

Blair didn't want to start any more fights with Tobin. She was trying to get laid.

Tobin entered the kitchen; he opened the refrigerator and took out a beer. Blair followed.

"Why you so worried about me?"

"Me...Worried? Not really."

Blair paused for a moment. She tried to convince herself she wasn't worried about him, but she wanted to know where he had been for the last few days. In the past, he would call her to let her know if he would be gone for a few days. He only did it as a courtesy, nothing more.

Seriously, where you been?" Blair leaned against the wall.

"I can't believe this, are you sure you wanna know?" He snickered.

Tobin came within inches of Blair's lips almost touching hers. She gasped. She wanted to feel his lips pressed against hers. She closed her eyes letting the smell of his cologne seep into her nose.

"I was out fucking another woman," he said with a laugh, and walked out of the kitchen.

Blair stood in the kitchen jolted by his words. That's not what she was expecting to hear. She followed him to his bedroom. He grabbed his gym bag; throwing his clothes into the bag.

"You going somewhere?" She asked getting in his face.

Tobin searched around his room, picking up more of his things and stuffing them into his bag, as Blair grabbed some of his clothes from the bag and threw them around the room.

"I can't do this." He paused, while Blair kept throwing his clothes everywhere.

"Well ain't this some shit!" She yelled.

"This isn't working. I'm moving out." Tobin remained calm. He didn't want Blair to get more out of control.

Tobin moved around the room, picking up his clothes and stuffing them back into the bag.

"Get the hell on then!" Blair raged.

Tobin continued to remain calm. He had never seen Blair this irate and wasn't sure what she was capable of.

"Don't worry about the rent money. I got you covered; I'll pay you for next month. One month should cover you until you find another roommate."

"Fuck that shit, fool! It ain't nothing; keep your stinkin' money, bitch ass!"

Blair stomped her foot and charged at Tobin. He didn't see it coming. He pushed her away, and she lunged at him again. They rolled on the floor. He wrestled her down and put his arm around her neck. He wasn't trying to choke her; he wanted her to calm down. She coughed.

"It's not worth it," he declared between breaths, as he let her go. "I'll be back to get the rest of my stuff." He grabbed his bag and left Blair on the floor.

"You're not going to fuck me whenever you want!" She screamed out.

"DRUNK SEX BLAIR!" He shouted from the living room. "That's what we had! DRUNKEN SEX."

"That drunken sex you kept wanting!" Blair met Tobin in the living room.

He rubbed his hands over his face. "You were lonely; I was lonely. We got drunk, and we had sex. That's it!" He picked his bag up off the floor; and walked to the front door.

"FUCK YOU!" Blair yelled.

Tobin slammed the door shut.

14

The next morning, Helen slammed pots and pans around the kitchen, still fired up over Sabrina's display of disrespect to the church and Ms. Doris. She burned breakfast and waited for Sabrina to come downstairs to the kitchen; Helen was ready to give Sabrina a piece of her mind. Charles ignored Helen, continuing to read his newspaper, and sip his coffee, when Trisha entered the kitchen.

"Have you seen Sabrina?" Helen asked Trisha.

"Well, good morning mother and how are you this morning?" Trisha sat at the breakfast bar.

"Trisha I don't want to hear any back talk from you this morning. Where's your sister?"

"She's gone."

Charles put his newspaper down and waited for Helen to explode.

"What do you mean; she's gone. Where did she go?" Helen slammed the frying pan on the stove.

"I don't know. I'd like my eggs scrambled hard. Hard. Not soft, not watery, but hard. And yeah, no bacon." Trisha replied.

Helen placed an empty plate in front of Trisha.

"No bacon because you haven't mastered bacon yet," Trisha winked at Helen.

Sabrina rarely went downtown. She parked her car at the New Carrollton subway station. The people on the subway intrigued her. The fat man who almost took up two seats and the small woman sitting next him trying to get comfortable; the loud high school kids talking about their weekends in what seemed like a foreign language, and the many business professionals pushing and shoving each other on and off the train trying to get to work on time.

Sabrina sat motionless as the train went from stop to stop; she listened for the train operator to call her station. Sabrina thought back to Dr. Kent's words of seeing adventure in her eyes and taking this trip downtown was like an adventure. This is so exciting!

The train operator called the next stop, Sabrina jumped out of her seat to stand at the doors. She didn't want to have to fight to get off the train. A bystander took her seat.

Once out of the subway, Sabrina wasn't sure which way to go to Dr. Kent's office building, many things had changed downtown. New buildings were standing where nothing had been previously, and old buildings got face-lifts. Everything was out of sorts.

Sabrina walked down the street; she walked back up the street, and as she turned to walk back down the street, she bumped into Tobin.

"Excuse me. I'm so sorry."

"No problem. Are you okay?"

Sabrina marveled at Tobin's good, rugged looks. His light hazel eyes startled her; it was like looking into the eyes of a cat. She almost caught herself staring into them before jerking herself back into reality.

"I'm a little lost."

"Where do you want to go?" he asked.

Sabrina handed Tobin the piece of paper with Dr. Kent's address.

"You're not too far, one block over. I'll be happy to show you if you like?"

Sabrina blushed at the thought of this handsome stranger wanting to help her.

"Oh...oh...no...no...I'm fine. Thanks for your help."

Sabrina took the paper back from Tobin and walked in the wrong direction. Tobin watched her walk up the street. Once Sabrina got to the end of the block, she realized she walked the wrong way. *I know he's probably looking at my back. How could I have been so stupid to walk the wrong way? Oh. My. God.*

Sabrina turned around and saw Tobin pointing in the opposite direction. She walked past him and pointed straight. He nodded and gave her a sweet smile.

Downtown Washington, DC - Connecticut Avenue and K Street

Sabrina arrived at the tall glass and mirrored office building; she looked up to see how far the building went into the sky. Many people went through the brass revolving door. She was shoved to the side as she entered the building from the people rushing in and out.

Sabrina went to the security desk and signed in. The officer on duty gave her directions to the elevators and the floor she needed to exit. From this point, she didn't have any trouble getting to the office. Once Sabrina arrived at Dr. Kent's office door, she paced back and forth. She walked away from the door. A woman came out and held the door for her.

"Are you going in?"

Sabrina nodded and entered the office and approached the receptionist desk. She looked around the lobby; two chairs lined each wall, with a small end table between one set of the chairs, and magazines sat on each table. What amazed Sabrina was; there weren't any patients. No one was in the lobby area.

Sabrina rang the bell. The smoky sliding glass window opened. A short chunky receptionist sat behind the glass window, smacking her gum. She didn't seem like the type of person Dr. Kent would've hired given Dr. Kent's style.

"Can I help you?" The receptionist asked in a thick southern accent.

"I have an appointment with Dr. Andrea Kent."

Sabrina rubbed her hands together and grabbed a tissue from the edge of the desk and she wiped her forehead. She wanted to flee, but she had come all this way.

This is where the adventure starts.

"Have you been here before?" The receptionist blew a bubble with her gum. It wasn't a big bubble, but between the smacking, the bubbles, and the thick country accent, Sabrina wanted to leave.

Standing firm, Sabrina answered, "No. I haven't."

The bubble pops. "Fill out these forms." The receptionist handed Sabrina a clipboard with medical forms, then closed the smoky sliding glass window.

She sat down and flipped through the forms attached to the clipboard. She wasn't unsure how to answer many of the blanks. She had never been to this kind of doctor.

Sabrina completed the forms and buzzed the receptionist. The smoky sliding glass window reopened, Sabrina gave the receptionist the clipboard, and she buzzed the side door open.

"Make a left. Kent's office is on the far right."

Sabrina entered the hall and made a left. She walked down a long hallway. She saw Dr. Kent's name on the far-right door. Her heart pounded. This was a mistake. She turned around to walk back down the hall, and the door opened. Dr. Kent walked out into the hall.

"Sabrina?"

Sabrina turned around.

"You caught me."

Dr. Kent motioned for her to come inside. Sabrina gradually walked in the office.

"I'm so glad you could come." Dr. Kent closed the office door. The sound of the lock clicking into the door horrified Sabrina. She was trapped.

"Have a seat."

Sabrina sat down on the sofa. Dr. Kent was an accomplished woman, many degrees and certificates hung on the wall. The bookshelf was filled with countless medical books and journals. Sabrina felt as if she was in capable hands.

"What can I help you with today?"

"I don't know what I'm doing here."

"Curiosity, maybe?

"Maybe."

"Sexual dysfunction is part of my practice, but I help people for a variety of reasons."

Is that why Deacon Byrd knew you so well?

"I see. Is that why Deacon Byrd came to see you?" Sabrina blurted out.

Dr. Kent moved from her chair and sat next to Sabrina, patting her on the knee. Sabrina moved her leg.

"Whatever gave you that impression Wallace wasn't a patient of mine. We were friends, nothing more, but if he was a patient, I wouldn't, I couldn't tell you anything. There are strict laws I must abide by regarding patient doctor confidentially."

"I assumed Deacon Byrd was seeing you as his doctor since you knew him so well."

"Psychologists are allowed to have friends," Dr. Kent said chuckling.

"Switching subjects, do you still live with your parents?"

"Why does that matter?" Sabrina snapped.

"I was asking you," Dr. Kent smiled.

The sweat dripped down Sabrina's back. She picked up a magazine off of the table and fanned herself.

"I do live with them."

Dr. Kent sensed Sabrina's nervousness. She wanted to make her comfortable. She switched topics again.

"Was Wallace an escape for you?"

"Wallace?" Sabrina didn't like how Dr. Kent used Deacon Byrd's first name. It was disrespectful to her, as his wife, even if she didn't want to be his wife. Sabrina thought there was more to the story than them being friends - Wallace.

"Deacon Byrd I mean." Dr. Kent restated.

"He was stable. I like stability."

"Seeing that Wall—Deacon Byrd has passed on, and you're a young vibrant woman; this is an opportunity for change." Dr. Kent handed Sabrina a flyer.

"I've seen this. I saw it at the lake posted to a tree."

"Marvelous. This is a different stable. I'm giving a speed dating event over at the Double Sky Bar and Lounge, and I want you to attend."

"No."

Dr. Kent's phone buzzed, "Excuse me." She answered the phone on the side table. "Sabrina, my next client is here. However, I want you to reconsider."

Baffled by Dr. Kent's statement; she chewed on the word client, and not patient. What was Dr. Kent up to?

Sabrina walked to the door.

"I won't." Sabrina left.

15

Tobin packed the rest of his belongings. He made sure the room was spotless, so Blair wouldn't have anything to complain about or have any reason to contact him. Before he could leave, Blair came home. She noticed Tobin's boxes and bags near the door. Blair went to Tobin's room and didn't notice Tobin's friend, Mike, sitting on the sofa.

"Well, well, what do we have here?"

"What does it look like?"

Blair sat down on the bed. "I didn't think you were serious. But you know how it goes."

Tobin ignored Blair. He grabbed the last bag and exited the bedroom. Blair followed.

"So this is it? This is how it ends?"

"Basically."

Tobin propped the front door open with a large box. He and Mike removed his stuff from the apartment.

Blair didn't want to make a scene with Mike there; she left them and went to her bedroom. She didn't know what else to do.

As she listened to them move his stuff out through the door, she bit her bottom lip hard, and didn't realize she had drawn blood.

16

*S*abrina and Trisha hadn't spent any time together since the death of Deacon Byrd. This was a good day for Sabrina to get back into the gym. She didn't have a membership, but Trisha invited her to hang out at the gym on campus. Trisha loved going to the gym, not because she wanted to be fit, but because of the benefits in meeting the men.

As Sabrina and Trisha jogged on the treadmill, they each ran quicker and quicker until Sabrina tripped.

"I won!" Trisha yelled.

Sabrina leaned over the side of the treadmill. She clutched the side, trying to catch her breath.

Breathe, breathe, and breathe.

Sabrina continued to breathe in and out heavily. She grabbed her knees.

"This is a first." Sabrina wiped the sweat from her forehead and around her neck.

Trisha put her hands in the air and shadow boxed like a fighter. "I am the greatest of all time." Trisha boasted in her best Muhammad Ali impersonation.

"Don't gloat!" Sabrina laughed.

Sabrina and Trisha sat on the floor and stretched. It was late at night, and no one was in the gym but a few gym rats near the weight machines and some women in the recreation room doing step aerobics.

"Ever done speed dating?" Sabrina tried to maintain an innocent look on her face. Trisha looked at Sabrina devilishly. Sabrina leaned up against the treadmill and stretched her calf. Trisha stood up and stretched her back.

"Been there, done that."

Sabrina gave Trisha a surprised look.

"Hell, you know I'll do anything once."

Trisha gave Sabrina her infamous wink and smile. The old man behind Sabrina thought it was for him. He grinned back, but of all days, he left his teeth at home.

Sabrina stood outside the Double Sky Bar and Lounge, near the new baseball stadium. The neon green OPEN sign lit the pathway to the entrance. Patrons entered and exited the bar. The Double Sky was rated one of the best after-work hour places to hang, by one of the DC city entertainment magazines. It was newly built when the federal government moved one of its major departments from the northwest side to the southwest side of the city.

Sabrina stood in front of the bar; she heard the laughter of the people standing outside the bar. She wasn't sure if they were laughing at her.

Sabrina decided it was best she left. She walked down the street and paused. She stood, in the distance, and looked at the bar. God, I know this is the opposite of what I know, but I need you to give me the strength to walk forward. I need one sign. Sabrina took a long pause before feeling her feet move forward. She walked back to the bar. She looked at her watch; the event was to begin in five minutes.

A group of women walked by Sabrina, laughing, but not at her. Each of the women were dressed in short dresses, baring a lot of skin.

Sabrina looked at her outfit, a long black skirt, white blouse with small ruffles down the front and one-inch heels. She stomped her foot and made weird noises as a tall handsome man bumped into her.

"Excuse me," he said in a deep baritone voice.

Sabrina's face brightened up.

The man entered the bar.

Thank you God. Sabrina followed.

Sabrina moved among the bar patrons and the crowd there for the speed dating event. She passed two men talking to two women also sitting at the bar. Sabrina looked around and clutched her purse.

As she continued to search for Dr. Kent among the crowded bar, Kelly, the speed dating event coordinator, approached her. Kelly eyed Sabrina from head to toe.

"You're not here for the Dr. Kent's speed dating event, are you?"

"Yes." Sabrina said with a sweet soft tone.

"You didn't register online, did you?"

Kelly walked around Sabrina in a circle eyeing her up and down. Sabrina tried to follow in her direction, but just turned in a circle.

"Register?"

"We're all booked, if you didn't register online."

"Is Dr. Kent here? She's the one that invited me."

Kelly laughed at Sabrina disrespectfully, "Dr. Kent invited us all sweetie."

"I see her," Sabrina snapped.

Sabrina walked through the crowd to Dr. Kent. Kelly tried double-timed her steps to reach Dr. Kent first. Once she reached

Dr. Kent, Kelly stepped in front of Sabrina to the right. Sabrina dodged around her by stepping to the left.

"Dr. Kent!" Kelly blurted out as Dr. Kent greeted Sabrina.

"Sabrina! I'm glad you could make it!"

Dr. Kent leaned over and gave Sabrina a kiss on each cheek.

"Never had that before," Sabrina uttered.

"Dr. Kent?" Kelly interrupted.

Dr. Kent moved pass Kelly. She walked Sabrina to the registration table. "I'm sure you'll have many of firsts."

Dr. Kent and Sabrina stood at the registration table as two blonde-haired women sitting at the table filled out their paperwork. Kelly stood by Dr. Kent like a lap dog waiting for her next set of instructions.

"Glad you changed your mind and came," Dr. Kent said. "Debbie will get you all set up. Kelly, you come with me." Dr. Kent and Kelly walked away from the registration table; Kelly turned to Sabrina and mumbled under her breath, "Bitch please," then smiled.

Blair and Donna, Blair's friend, and coworker at the Double Sky, sat on the wine boxes in the backroom of the bar.

Unlike Blair, Donna Danson grew up in Northwest, Washington, DC, near 16th Street off the Gold Coast. Donna came from a well-to-do family. Her parents sent her to private schools and paid for her college education. She received her degree in Art History but couldn't find a job due to the recession and the high unemployment rate. In her late twenties, Donna did what she had to do to survive, she worked as a stripper in a bar in Waldorf, but the money got so good to her; she'd spend it on clothing, handbags, and trips. When her parents found out about her stripping job, they threw her out of the house. She wanted to go back to school to get her master's degree, but as fast as the money came, she spent it even faster. Blair helped Donna get a job at the Double Sky to help her stay focused on school. Blair figured if she was a loss cause didn't mean everyone had to be one. She felt like she had to help Donna because no one helped her.

"Hell, I should try to find a man, Dr. Kent out did herself this time," Donna remarked while taking a drag of her cigarette.

"I didn't even notice."

Donna had never seen Blair looking this down. Blair was the one who dumped men, not the other way around.

"Girl, get over Tobin, get out there and find someone."

"I'm not even in the mood. Truth be told, I've never met anyone like Tobin. When he first moved in, he would play the new songs he wrote. We'd hang out, chill out and get drunk; nothing major. Until we slept together. That's when he got shitty."

"You knew he wasn't into you like that."

Donna tried to warn Blair from the jump, don't let Tobin's good looks interfere with her judgment; he only wanted some noncommittal ass, nothing more. Blair wouldn't listen. She thought she had the upper hand. It backfired on her and now her emotions were committed to having Tobin.

"I couldn't tell he blew my back out. I'm getting goose bumps, Just thinking about it!" Blair rubbed her hand across her arms.

"Tobin was stuck up; you didn't see it."

"Whatever."

"I know stuck up when I see it, hell, I'm stuck up. Stuck up knows the stuck fuck up!" Donna laughed.

Blair wasn't in the mood for Donna's jokes. "Being jealous doesn't suit you." Blair drew one last puff on her cigarette then left.

"Was it something I said?" Donna snickered.

Blair returned to the bar. The crowd was still thick from the event, and orders were coming in left and right. Blair was thankful for the help from the other bartender. She knew she wouldn't have been able to mix all those drinks alone. Donna too was busy. But not too busy, to notice something interesting in the far corner of the bar and lounge.

"Did you know Tobin was here?" Donna teased Blair.

"I don't have time for any of your bullshit tonight, Donna!"

"I'm not kidding! I saw Tobin; he's taking part in the speed dating event." Donna pointed to Tobin in the far-right corner. "Believe or not, he's here."

Blair moved from behind the bar, to get a closer look; and in the corner was Tobin, talking to a light-skinned woman, who kept smiling and giggling. Blair returned to the bar. She paced.

"Whatever you have on your mind; you better let it go; this is not the place." Donna said.

Blair remained calm. She knew this wasn't the place to cause a scene. But when she got a chance, she would ask him about it.

Tobin hoped this wouldn't set Blair off any further; but this was his way of sending her a clear-cut message - that there was nothing between them. Blair had been calling him non-stop; leaving her rants and fits of rage on his voicemail.

Sabrina glimpsed Tobin, but the Double Sky was dimly lit where he and his companion sat. Sabrina didn't pay him any attention.

Contrary to what Donna thought, Tobin was not participating in the speed-dating event. He asked his cousin out for dinner since she was in town.

Sabrina approached Dawn, the speeding dating registrar. "Is there anything for Sabrina Sloan?"

Dawn checked through the full stack of papers. She double-checked.

"I'm sorry; I don't seem to have anything for you, but we get late forms." Debbie tried to reassure Sabrina.

Sabrina nodded her head, but she knew there weren't any late forms.

It was later than usual for Sabrina to be out. Her car was parked down the street and from the distance; she could see the streetlight was out. She turned around to see if anyone was following as she ran to her car. Pulling out her keys, she pushed the remote, got into her car, and locked the doors.

Sabrina beat her head on the steering wheel as her eyes welled up.

"What the hell was I thinking? Look at the way I'm dressed!" She screamed out. Sabrina continued to hit her hands against the steering, just when Blair knocked on the driver's side window.

"AAAAAAHHHHHH." Her heart pounded from Blair knocking on her window. Blair motioned Sabrina to roll down her window, but Sabrina refused.

"I saw you at the bar!"

Sabrina shook her head.

"You were at the Double Sky for the speed dating event!

Sabrina cracked the window - slightly.

"You came from the Double Sky Bar and Lounge. I saw you. I'm the bartender there."

Sabrina rolled the window down. "I'm sorry. I'm usually not out this late." Sabrina wiped her face.

"I saw you in the speed dating event tonight. I knew you weren't a regular you looked out of place."

"What a waste of time."

"I think I can help you."

Blair lit a cigarette and slipped Sabrina a piece of paper with her number; she blew the smoke out into the night air.

"Give me a call."

Sabrina accepted the paper with Blair's number and then drove away.

"Lawd, that girl needs help." Blair said.

17

Sabrina tossed and turned in her bed. She sat up and looked around her bedroom. The clock read three in the morning. She thought about how bad the speed-dating event went. She never thought her life would be this boring. Some of the men she met at the event were interesting, but none of them peaked her interest. And it was obvious she didn't peak theirs. Sabrina didn't understand why she even cared that she bombed out at the event. One man she met lived in his mother's basement, the other just got out of jail for driving while drunk, and the one she liked the most - the investment banker, was uptight and more concerned with his looks than getting to know her.

Sabrina grabbed her cell phone and texted Blair. She knew it was late, but she figured a woman like Blair stayed up late. Sabrina decided she needed all the help she could get. The excitement rose in her stomach when Blair texted back and said she'd help.

~

Sabrina watched her parents from the entrance of the kitchen, just like any other morning; Helen prepared breakfast, with smoke coming from the stove; Charles read his newspaper and sipped his coffee. She didn't like her parents being so predictable. Every morning Helen concocted plates of food no one wanted to eat, and Charles only drank his coffee and read his newspaper. She figured her life was boring because she got it from her parents. Sabrina was convinced her parents would die in the kitchen.

"Well, look who joined us?" Helen didn't expect an answer.

"Your biscuits are burning." Sabrina shot back with a dry tone.

"I mean really! When can we get a decent meal around this camp? Trisha fanned the smoke, trying to save the biscuits.

"You were out late last night, Sabrina." Charles interjected.

Sabrina stood in awe of her father contributing to the morning discussion.

"She went to a single's event last night." Trisha chimed in.

"A what!"

Sabrina rolled her eyes and waited for them on slot of verbal abuse. Helen may have been Christian, but that never stopped her from telling anyone what was on her mind.

"That's what I call progress." Trisha insisted.

"Thanks, blabber mouth."

Sabrina reached for the classified section of the newspaper. She drank her juice, tucked the newspaper under her arm and left.

"Trisha, have you been teaching your sister your wicked ways?"

"It was bound to happen," Charles concluded.

"Chaaarles!"

Charles looked over the rim of his glasses and snorted with his laughter.

∽

"So how was it?" Trisha asked.

"A disaster; plus, you didn't have let worrywart know I went."

Trisha walked out of the house on her way down the street as Sabrina followed to her car.

"I hope you didn't wear one of your tired ass church outfits."

I did! Sabrina didn't say anything to Trisha, but somehow, she knew Trisha already knew what happened.

"Besides, where are you going?" Sabrina asked.

"Anytime you need some help, you know I've got your back! I'm going to play one on one with the guy down the street."

"Why do I get the feeling that has nothing to do with basketball?"

Trisha jumped through the waterspout and let the water sprinkle on her. The gardeners across the street stopped planting to admire Trisha as she got wet.

Sabrina drove off.

Sabrina located Blair's apartment building on 49th Street Northeast.

"Come on in. I'm so glad you text me." Blair said, answering the door.

"Me too."

Blair shut the door and led Sabrina to the living room. Donna sat on the sofa eating. Blair cut the television off.

"Heeey...I was watching that!"

"Donna — Sabrina, Sabrina — Donna."

Sabrina held her hand out. Donna wiped her hands on her jeans. They shook hands.

"Sorry, hands are a little greasy."

"Donna works at the Double Sky with me; I'd say she knows me best."

Blair tossed Sabrina a towel to wipe her hands; Sabrina took a seat on the sofa next to Donna. Blair plopped down in the beanbag chair on the floor. Blair tilted her head to the side and stared at Sabrina.

"I think we should start with your hair."

Sabrina ran her hand through her ponytail, "What's wrong with my hair?

Donna reached over to touch Sabrina's ponytail, and Sabrina jerked away.

The LAST thing I need is your onion ring grease in my hair! Who does that? Just puts their greasy hands in someone's hair?

Donna could see how annoyed Sabrina was by her actions.

"Nothing's wrong with it, if you are a pony." Donna said.

"Or if you're a kid." Blair laughed. "Ponytails are for kids and not for attracting a man."

"But you're wearing a ponytail." Sabrina said innocently to Blair.

"She can't stop wearing a ponytail." Donna said.

"Well, I'm not looking for a man, now, am I?" Blair stated, "I have a man."

Donna laughed. "You do?"

Sabrina wasn't sure what was going between Blair and Donna, but it sounded like someone wasn't telling the truth. She didn't know either of them well enough to say which one. There was something definitely off about each of them.

"Never mind her, jealousy is her middle name." Blair said.

Blair rolled on the floor and then hopped up to go to the kitchen. From the kitchen, the blender roared. Sabrina walked around the apartment. She thumbed through a magazine about tattoos. She looked through Blair's collection of compact disks, and before she could finish looking through them, Blair came out of the kitchen with a tray of mixed drinks.

"You're gonna need a complete makeover." Blair continued without missing a beat.

Blair handed Sabrina a drink. Sabrina declined. Donna grabbed her drink from the tray.

"I insist."

"I gotta admit Blair makes the best drinks on this side of town."

"All over town fool!"

Sabrina reconsidered and accepted the drink.

"You remind me so much of my sister," Sabrina sipped the drink. She spat it out and frowned. "Oh my, what is that?" She wiped the liquid from her chin.

"Something I made; it's called the Bully."

"A bully?"

"No, the Bully," Blair said.

"Like a bully in the backyard. Blair won't tell me what's in it." Donna took another sip, "but whatever it is, I love it."

Blair spilled some of the drink on her shirt as she sat down, "It's my specialty drink. Please don't tell me you don't drink either."

"No, I don't drink."

"You'll be drinking in no time hanging with Blair."

"You're gonna need a COMPLETE makeover!"

Sabrina took another sip of the Bully. She snorted as she laughed. Blair laughed. They all rose their glasses for a toast.

"Here's to makeovers!" Blair yelled out.

"Makeovers!" Sabrina and Donna shouted back.

18

*D*owntown, Washington DC - Foggy Bottom

If Sabrina would make a complete change, there were certain things she would need. Hair, makeup, and clothing would cost her loads money, and because she was only Deacon Byrd's wife for six hours at the most, the first family felt a hundred dollars an hour was sufficient compensation for her time. She didn't even fight them on it.

She set up interviews with three companies. She didn't have many specialized skills, but she was decent with office work, and she had her associate degree in business. Sabrina wasn't sure if Ms. Doris would give her a good reference after her quitting fiasco; so, she put Minister Byrd on her resume. The last time Sabrina saw Ms. Doris at church, steam still blew from her ears.

By chance, Sabrina got the job with the first interview. It was the one she wanted the most. The same day, the office manager escorted Sabrina to her cubicle and showed her the ropes. Ecstatic to sit down, Sabrina looked through the drawers and smiled the entire time as the office manager trained her.

~

Sabrina knew another speed-dating event was coming up soon. She had to look the part, act the part and be the part. The goal was to blast all the competition away. Sabrina met Blair at the Tulay Hair Salon on Wisconsin Avenue; it was the most upscale hair salon in the city specializing in ethnic hair. Sabrina had never heard of Tulay, but Blair was good friends with the head stylist, a gay male, named Chauncey "The Danger" Ranger. Blair bartended some of his hair show events and she told Sabrina how exotic the crowd was, but if she was serious about making a change, he was the expert.

Chauncey frowned at Sabrina's hair. He sashayed to the left, and then to the right in his red tight skinny Abercrombie & Fitch slacks, accented with a shimmery gold ruffled shirt he wore slightly open to show off his freshly waxed chest. He even had the nerve to wear pure white Italian leather loafers with no socks. Sabrina saw it as strange, and stylish, but he pulled it off well. She had never met anyone as enlightening as him.

He forced Sabrina into his style chair, rubbed his hands together, and then spun her around.

What does this fool think he's about to do to my hair?

"This is so wrong darling," he said with a long drag of agony in his British accent, "Blair baby what have you brought me?" He stomped one foot.

Before Blair could answer, Chauncey interjected, "A mess baby, just a mess," he sighed.

"What can do you for her?"

Chauncey switched his little ass in his little pants and twirled around Sabrina. He put his finger on his chin, "this broad needs color, some trim - not poohnannie," he giggled at his own amusement, "her ends are rough, and we ain't talkin' about money honey."

Sabrina sat in the chair in silence. She didn't know how to react to Chauncey's displeasure.

"Before you go overboard sweetie, can we do something conservative?"

Yes, conservative is good...I think. I can't have it both ways. Can I?

Chauncey gasped. "Honey, I'm THEE DANGER RANGER," he said, as he used air quotes," dangerous and fierce on any runway," he snapped his fingers. "We don't do ordinary Blair baby, you know this!"

Sabrina could feel The Danger Ranger's agitation. Blair didn't want to stifle his creativity, just tone it down for a person like Sabrina; she wasn't ready for anything too dramatic.

"Can ya do extraordinary with less extra?" Blair quipped.

"Moon muffin, trust me, this one is like a blank canvas." Chauncey tousled Sabrina's hair; looked her in her eyes, "your face is cute as a cumquat, and your wardrobe is short bus, but I can fix that too."

Moon muffin and cute as a cumquat? What is this dude smoking?

Sabrina made an ugly face at the thought of Chauncey helping her with the wardrobe. He didn't seem like the person who would wear anything that remotely matched.

Sabrina had no idea what was about to happen to her long black locks. She never had it cut or colored; she wore a ponytail all her life, but she was ready to make the change.

When Chauncey revealed Sabrina's new haircut, Blair knew this was it. Sabrina had the best Halle Berry pixie cut she had ever seen.

Trisha thought it was good idea for Sabrina to try out her new look. Plus, she wanted to take her out before Helen got a chance to see. Trisha knew once Helen saw how Sabrina cut all her hair off, she was good as dead.

Trisha dressed Sabrina in one of her outfits and took her sister to one of her weeknight hangouts, the Smoky Bar and Grill in Bowie, not far from where they lived. They also had a pool hall in the back, for a dollar a game and Trisha liked to hustle the men for drinks.

Tonight, Trisha hung back and watch the scene. It was Sabrina's nightlife debut. She ordered them two drinks, and it wasn't before long two nice-looking men approached them.

"Can we buy you ladies something to drink?" The first dude asked.

"Sure." Trisha said.

He motioned to the bartender to come over.

"What can I get ya?"

"Whatever the ladies want," he said.

The second dude scanned Sabrina, giving her a seductive eye Sabrina didn't notice.

"My name is Chris," the second dude said to Sabrina, "Is it the two of you here tonight?"

Sabrina slurped her rest of her drink from a straw; it made noises. Trisha kicked Sabrina underneath the bar.

Why in the hell is she kicking me?

"Ouch! What did you do that for?" Sabrina yelled.

"That depends." Trisha responded.

Trisha never realized how out of touch Sabrina was to nightlife. She didn't have any sophistication. No matter what outfit she had on or what kind of hairstyle she rocked, Sabrina still had church chick written across her forehead like a marquee. But Trisha knew, even the best of the church chicks had naughty chick in them too.

"Dance?" The dude asked Trisha.

"Sure, what's your name?"

"Tom."

Trisha incited Tom on to the small dance floor with her sexy moves. Sabrina hung back and watched them dance. Tom placed his hands-on Trisha's lower back and pulled her closer, they swayed to the music; Sabrina swayed in her chair.

"Damn, whatever was in that glass, I love it!" Sabrina shouted.

The alcohol crept up Sabrina's spine; the warmth incased her body. She took off the short leather jacket she borrowed from her sister and fanned herself.

The bartender placed two new drinks on the bar. Sabrina attacked the medium-size glass with the brown liquid.

"Give me more of that, chief!"

"I don't have a boyfriend." She burped and then giggled.

"I see. I think you're finished, let me refresh that for you. What are you having?" He took the glass from her.

"How he gonna strip me of my glass like that, it still had a corner!" Sabrina pouted, "I don't know what this is;" Sabrina's glossy eyes followed the glass as Chris gave it to the bartender." My sister ordered it." She hiccupped.

The bartender approached Chris." The lady will have what her sister ordered."

"Rum and Coke?" The bartender confirmed.

"Rum and coke it is. So --"

Sabrina grabbed the drink from the bartender when he returned.

"So...do you wanna dance?"

Chris turned to see his friend getting freaky with Trisha on the dance floor. He wondered if could see action.

No, you ain't getting any ass tonight!

"No, not really." Sabrina stayed glued to her bar stool and listened to the music.

~

Chris sped up to the front of the Sloan house. Sabrina tripped out of the front seat of his car and crawled her way to the sidewalk.

"Thank you," she slurred.

I am fucked up!

The car made a loud screeching noise as Chris raced off down the street, barely allowing the wind to close the door. Sabrina stumbled through the bushes and up the hilly lawn. She imagined she was dancing in a ballet, but if anyone was looking, she was dancing with the air. Just as soon as Sabrina went to do a pirouette, she fell on her face on to the grass laughing, and then she passed out.

A few moments later, Tom and Trisha pulled up in front of the house in his expensive two-seater sports car, when they made out. Tom opened his eyes, and looked over Trisha's shoulder, and spotted Sabrina passed out on the lawn.

"I think that's your sister."

Trisha continued to kiss his face.

"What...huh..."

He pulled away from her.

"Your sister...she's passed out on the front lawn."

Trisha eyeballed Sabrina curled up on the lawn like a baby.

"Shit. Let me get her before my mother sees her." They kissed again for a few more minutes. Trisha had to pry herself away from him.

"Do you need some help?"

"I'm cool."

They kissed one more time before Trisha exited the car. Once she reached Sabrina, she struggled to lift her off the lawn.

"What the hell have you been eating?"

Feeling the pulling and dragging from Trisha, Sabrina woke up.

"Huh? I — I think Imma throw up!"

Sabrina ran to the corner of the house and vomited.

19

*B*lair picked up her iPhone; she had been drinking and smoking for most of the night. Darkness filled the apartment. The only light illuminating the walls came from the streetlamp outside.

She clicked the red button on her iPhone in the middle of dialing Tobin. She wanted to call him. The last time she saw him was at the Double Sky, the night of the speed-dating event.

She caught herself at a moment of vulnerability. Blair always wanted to appear as if she didn't need anyone for any reason. She figured she had made it this far without family or many friends, and she'd continue to make it.

She hung up the phone and looked out the window at the night sky.

Tobin and Mike drank their beers while cartoons blasted from the television, and Mike's kids watched.

"Does Blair still call you?"

Tobin took another sip of beer. "Don't mention her name! I don't wanna talk that crazy bitch up!"

The kids circle around Tobin's chair singing, "CRAZY BITCH! CRAZY BITCH! CRAZY BITCH!"

"Damn, man! Watch your fucking language! Don't you see my kids are here?"

Tobin shot Mike a weird glance.

20

*T*risha gave Sabrina a cup of instant coffee. "You're gonna need this now."

"My head," Sabrina moaned.

"Drink up, you have a hangover."

Trisha left the kitchen as Sabrina sat at the breakfast bar rubbing her temples. She ran her hands through her hair massaging her scalp hoping it would relieve the pounding pain. I don't think I'm ever going to do this again.

She gently placed the warm mug around her eyes.

Helen came downstairs to see what the commotion was in the kitchen crossing paths with Sabrina as she tried to go upstairs. Helen grabbed her wrist. Sabrina winched. Oh, shit here we go.

"Why would you cut your beautiful long hair?" She held Sabrina's wrist tighter.

"Aren't you a little late?" Sabrina slurred.

"Have you been drinking?" Helen sniffed Sabrina. "I expected this behavior from Trisha, but not you."

Sabrina yanked her wrist free from Helen's death grip.

I swear this woman is gonna make me knock her ass out!

Sabrina giggled. Damn, I'm drunk. She needs to pray on it. Please Lord, help me, this could get ugly.

"I don't understand you anymore." Helen agonized.

Sabrina paused on the stairs. She hung her head low.

I knew my mother's feelings were hurt, but there was no turning back. I wanted adventure in my life; and if she was upset, so be it.

"Well, maybe it's not your job anymore to understand me. This is the new me." Sabrina sighed. "Well, not the me right now...but the me I will be tomorrow." Sabrina chuckled.

Lord, help me from laughing at this. Sabrina held her hand over her mouth like a child.

Helen didn't know what to make of Sabrina's behavior, she wanted to snatch her by what was left of her hair and drag her to see the minister.

"What has gotten into you?" Helen asked.

Sabrina rolled her eyes and threw her hands up in the air as she disappeared up the stairs.

Nearby, Trisha listened, "Rum and coke, ma. Nothing but rum and coke has gotten into her!" she hollered.

$\mathcal{W}$hile Sabrina waited for Dr. Kent, she thumbed through a magazine on the table. She looked at her watch and paced around the room. She noticed a file cabinet in the corner, with the bottom drawer slightly open. Sabrina searched around the room looking for a hidden camera. This is mumbo jumbo; she can't possibility have a hidden camera in here; that's against patient confidentiality rules.

Sabrina tugged on the top drawer; it opened a little; Sabrina pulled it again to open it all the way. She skimmed the file folders; they were patient files. She rummaged around for the letter B. She went through each folder looking for Deacon Byrd's name. She switched to the second drawer. Deacon Byrd's folder wasn't there. Sabrina closed both file drawers, just as Dr. Kent rushed into the office. She quickly moved over to the bookshelf and pretended to read the spines of the medical books.

"I'm sorry; I'm late," Dr. Kent said, "My other patient took longer than expected." Dr. Kent went behind her desk and straightened her clothing.

Sabrina sat down in the chair instead of the sofa and crossed her legs. Dr. Kent observed Sabrina's behavior; and saw the bottom drawer to the file cabinet slightly open.

"What brings you here today?"

"When are you giving another speed dating event?"

"You didn't need to make an appointment to ask me that."

Sabrina squirmed in her seat. She crossed her legs the other way turning her back away from Dr. Kent.

Dr. Kent stood over Sabrina's chair for a moment. Sabrina noticed the bottom drawer was open.

"I didn't meet anyone, but I'm willing to try again." Sabrina tried to stay on the topic, hoping Dr. Kent wouldn't notice the file cabinets. But the good doctor saw and leaned against the cabinet.

Sabrina smiled.

Dr. Kent closed the file cabinet with her foot and locked it. Sabrina grabbed a handful of candy from the open candy dish. Dr. Kent moved in closer. Does she know?

"Is there something else you want to tell me Sabrina, or do I have to pull out the tape from my hidden camera?" Dr. Kent suggested as her eyes widen.

"Nmm...ooo. Not at the mo...me...nt," Sabrina stuttered as her words drifted. I could just pee on myself.

"I was just joking." Dr. Kent laughed." Here's the next speed-dating event, hosted by a friend of mine." She handed her the flyer from off the table. "I'm so glad you're making a new life for yourself."

The color from Sabrina's face went directly into the pit of her stomach. Her hands shook as she accepted the flyer; her leg went in an up and down motion, breathing heavily as if the air was being sucked from her lungs. Get yourself together Sabrina, she doesn't know for real.

"Are you okay?"

"I'm fine," she said with a weak smile. "I must leave now."

As soon as, Sabrina got on the train, she couldn't relax. I didn't mean to snoop, but I wanted to know what kind of relationship, she and Deacon Byrd had. *Does she know I'm lying?*

Sabrina closed her eyes and let the motion of the train rock her to sleep. Once at the New Carrollton Metro Station, she still felt guilty for digging into Dr. Kent's patient files. *How will I ever be able to look her in the eyes ever again?*

22

---

*S*abrina and Trisha drove in to the Bowie Town Center Starbucks. They searched for a parking space close by.

For Sabrina going to Starbucks was a treat. Trisha shook if she didn't have her daily dose of the liquid crack. She loved the way it smelled while being brewed. Sabrina tried to get Trisha to make it at home, but she said it didn't taste the same. When it came to Starbucks, Trisha budgeted a portion of her weekly paycheck to her Starbucks purchases.

Sabrina and Trisha made it into the store, just before a long line formed. This Starbucks was a nice size; inside they had circle tables, each table having at least two chairs, and in the back, lounge chairs and sofas for people to set up their laptops to hang out.

"I did something out of character," Sabrina said.

"You've been doing a lot of things out of character these days."

"I snooped through Dr. Kent's confidential patient records." Guilt encompassed Sabrina's face.

"What did you do that for? And why were you at Dr. Kent's anyway?"

Shit, I've opened a can of worms now. I don't feel like explaining all of this to her. Should have never opened by big mouth! "Never mind all that, just know I was there." Sabrina deflected the conversation. "I think Deacon Byrd was having an affair with her."

"Ewww, that's nasty...on Dr. Kent's part!"

"Tell me about it." Sabrina shivered. "She wasn't in the office, and I saw one of the file cabinets was open, so I had me a look see."

"What did you find?"

"Nothing. And then she almost caught me!"

"Don't you know by now, if they were seeing each other, she wouldn't keep patient records on it."

Trisha brushed Sabrina off while she ordered her a Venti Cappuccino, Extra Dry. "You getting something?"

"Nah, I'm not in the mood now." Damn she's right. What the hell was I thinking? Why would she keep those kinds of records? He wasn't a patient, she said he was a friend, but why can't I believe?

Sabrina read the flyer Dr. Kent gave her. She registered for the event online and received her conformational email. Sabrina looked in her closet. She tossed skirts and blouses out.

Sabrina busted into Trisha's room.

"I need help!"

Trisha continued to paint her nails.

"Help with what?"

Trisha fanned her toenails. Sabrina turned the radio down.

"I need an outfit. Ihavenothingtowearanthespeeddatingeventis-comingup," Sabrina uttered in one breath.

Trisha walked on her heels to her closet. She dug out a pair of black skinny slacks by MICHAEL Michael Kors, a white and navy Equipment 'Daddy' tie front shirt, with a pair of loafers made my Coach.

No wonder she's always broke.

"An outfit." Trisha walked back to her spot.

Sabrina fumbled through the clothes.

"Let me hook up your makeup, and you're set."

Sabrina tried on the clothing to see how they would look. Trisha then experimented with different hairstyles on Sabrina. As Sabrina marveled in the mirror at the hook up, her cell phone rang.

"Hello?" She paused. "Sure. I'm on my way."

She hung up the phone.

"Who was that on the phone?"

None of your business.

Sabrina changed back into her jeans and shirt.

"You straight?" Trisha asked.

"I'll tell you later."

Trisha shooed Sabrina out of her room as she gathered the items and departed.

Sabrina didn't want to tell Trisha; but Blair invited her to come hang out at the Double Sky. Trisha would have wanted to tag along, and Sabrina thought this was her adventure, not she and Trisha's adventure. Plus, she wanted to do something different; she didn't want her younger sister hanging around giving her competition.

As usual, the Double Sky was jammed with people; standing room only, dance floor oozing with lustful young women and men, looking to get a hit for the night. It always amazed Sabrina how the Double Sky could cater to the professional crowd during the day, but by ten at night; it would be a nightclub.

Sabrina searched for Blair behind the bar as she wadded through the crowd. Blair glimpsed Sabrina, she whistled for her to come over. Once they locked eyes, Sabrina waved as Blair continued to serve up the drinks. Sabrina squeezed through the sardines of people standing at the bar. She could only stand sideways.

"Glad you could make it!"

Sabrina bobbed her head to the music.

"Is everything okay? You sounded out of sorts on the phone."

"I'm cool, just thought you'd like to hang out."

Blair served Sabrina one of her specialty drinks, the Tight End. Sabrina didn't have any clue what was in it, but whatever it was; Sabrina felt the need to unbutton a few of her buttons on her shirt.

As Sabrina nursed the Tight End, a man with better looks than Bradley Cooper approached her.

"Hi, my name is Shawn, wanna dance?"

Sabrina looked around for someone who could be behind her and then pointed to herself. Before she could say no, he flashed a smile. Wow look at how perfect his teeth are! What the hell!

Sabrina nodded, and they headed to the dance floor. Blair looked on. She knew this was a good thing for Sabrina, even if she paid the dude to ask her to dance. Sabrina and Shawn danced for most of the night while Blair kept sending Sabrina drinks by Donna. She kept them light knowing Sabrina wasn't an experienced drinker.

"I had a nice time; can I have your number?" Shawn asked while walking back to the bar.

"Sure." Sabrina's eyes lit up like the lights on a Christmas tree. No man ever asked her for her number. Sabrina wrote her cell phone number, he kissed on her the cheek; she blushed.

He is sexy as hell. Yummy! Sabrina giggled.

"Thanks for nice night."

"No problem."

Shawn left Sabrina sitting at the end of the bar spinning around in the chair. He called Blair over to the side, "Keep your money; she was fun," he said, and then he left.

Blair shot Sabrina thumbs up.

The sun shone on Sabrina's face through the window. She tried to block it with her palm. She moaned, tossed, and turned. Her lower back ached as she noticed she was on Blair's sofa. Her cell phone lying on the floor rang. She groaned as she sat up, arching her back and running her hands through her hair. She peeped at the cell phone caller ID, groaned, and then ignored it, prior to turning it off. Sabrina rose from the sofa to step over Donna curled up on the floor cuddling a bottle of Red Berry Ciroc.

Sabrina stumbled into the bathroom, knelt, gripped the edge of the toilet, and hung her head over it. Whatever was in her stomach, all came up.

Helen hung up the phone. She paced the kitchen. Charles entered the kitchen when Helen dove at him and grabbed his shirt. The tears came down her face.

"I don't know where she is. Where could she be? Has she gone crazy? Am I a bad mother? This is the devil's work." Helen rambled on.

Charles glanced at the bare table. "Helen? Where's my coffee? Where's my paper?" Pulling her off his shirt.

Helen let go. She picked up the phone again and dialed the number; it went to voicemail.

"Sabrina didn't come home last night."

"And?"

"Her phone was ringing, now it's going to her voicemail."

Trisha caught the tail end of Helen's tirade as she entered the kitchen.

"She turned it off. Maaaaa, where's breakfast?"

"What do you mean it's turned it off? Your sister didn't come home last night!"

"What does that have to do with MY breakfast?"

By the time, Helen was beside herself. She felt like the devil was in her house trying to take over.

"Doesn't anyone give a rat's ass what is wrong with Sabrina?" Helen grabbed the pan and slammed it on the stove. "You want breakfast; fix it your damn self! The damn newspaper is on the porch!"

Helen left Charles and Trisha in the kitchen.

"She's snapped." Trisha said calmly.

Charles thought so too.

"TRRRRIIIISSSSHAAAA, I heard that! Don't make me hurt you!" Helen screeched from the living room.

Sabrina turned her phone back on, and it rang again.

"Hello mother." She paused. "I'm fine mother. I'll be home soon." Sabrina hung up the cell phone and plopped back on the sofa.

Helen sat next to the phone in the living room." She hung up on me!" She yelled.

Charles kneeled in front of Helen, he held her hand; he kissed it. "Now you've spoken to her, can I get my coffee and paper please?"

"Your oldest child is being swept away by the devil, and you don't care!"

Trisha stood in the archway between the living room and vestibule. "You cursed us out; I would think the devil is sweeping you first! Ma, chill out! Sabrina is grown. It's about time she experiences life."

"Being a harlot like you doesn't make up experiencing life!"

Trisha took three steps to Helen ready to pounce on her, but she knew if she did, that was her ass. "Kick rocks Helen!" Trisha said, as she stormed out; that was the best she could do and still stay alive.

"What? Kick what? Charles, did you hear what she said?" Helen gasped. "That's devil speak! Who kicks rocks?" Helen was confused.

"Did you have to call her a harlot?" Charles left Helen in the living room by herself. "I'll get my own damn coffee."

Helen sat alone; the room became dark as tears encompassed her eyes. She felt like her family was falling apart, and she didn't know how to stop it. The devil was taking over.

Sabrina entered the house through the back porch door, hoping to avoid any contact with Helen. She figured by the time she came in everyone would be out of the kitchen, but to her surprise, Helen stood at the sink washing dishes.

Helen heard the back door slam, and she knew it was Sabrina.

She stopped washing dishes, stood silently, and looked out the window. Sabrina walked through the kitchen.

I thought about speaking, but why? I wasn't in the mood for any of Helen's antics. Plus, I have a monster headache.

Helen continued to wash dishes as Sabrina exited the kitchen just as she entered.

23

To get out of the house, Sabrina invited Trisha, Blair, and Donna to the mall. Her wardrobe still didn't meet the standards she had in mind for her transformation. They drove out to Tyson's Corner.

Walking around the mall, Trisha entered Victoria Secret.

"There are more men In here than women." Donna noticed.

"I hope whatever they are copping; they are getting something for the wife too." Blair laughed.

"Thongs are horrible." Sabrina added, as she picked up one and held it high for everyone to see.

"What? Thongs make sure don't have a panty line!" Trisha interjected. "I see we have a lot of work to do, where did I go wrong?"

Everyone laughed, but Sabrina, "I don't find that funny!"

"Here buy these and let's move on." Blair handed Sabrina few pairs of hip huggers and cheekies in polka dots, pink, purple and black.

"How am I supposed to cover my butt in these?"

"Your ass won't be in them long enough for it to be covered!" Blair refuted.

"It was never about your ass!" Donna added.

Trisha cut in and handed Sabrina a different pair of underwear. "Here throw these boy shorts in for good measure."

Sabrina knew the girls were right; she needed to stop fighting it every step of the way, but change wasn't easy. She purchased the selections and was ready to move on to the next store.

As they left Victoria's Secret, they walked throughout the mall in and out of various stores.

"I'm hungry; let's get a bite to eat in the eatery." Donna suggested.

They walked around looking for something to eat.

"I'll get us a table," Blair said.

Blair walked around looking for a table, in the distance, she saw Tobin eating with a female companion. She stood still; her feet would not allow her to move.

"I thought you were looking for a table," Donna said, "Now, I have my bags, my tray, and nowhere to sit."

Blair held her ground and didn't move.

"What has gotten into you? Table? Food? My drink is about to spill!"

Sabrina and Trisha joined Blair and Donna. Blair continued not to move; her eyes fixated on Tobin, in the distance, laughing with a young blonde-haired woman. Donna finally noticed what Blair saw.

"We've gotta go." Donna tried to push Blair long; despite all the things, she had in her hands.

Sabrina looked over in the direction where Blair was looking, but she didn't know exactly what or where Blair was looking.

"What's going on?" Trisha asked.

"That's my boyfriend over there with that girl."

"They could be coworkers. It is lunch time," Sabrina said.

Sabrina looked for another table on the other side of the eatery. She didn't notice Tobin's face. Donna forced Blair to move.

"This is not the time or place to make a scene," Donna mentioned.

Sabrina and Trisha didn't know the actual situation between Blair and Tobin, and it wasn't Donna's place to tell either of them, the real deal.

Before Donna could stop Blair, Blair marched over to Tobin's table.

The young blonde-haired woman sat at the table giggling. The woman sat close enough to Tobin to rub her hands on his back. He smiled at her and then tapped her nose. Just as soon as the young blonde-haired woman went to kiss Tobin, Blair stood at the table.

"Boooooy you sure like to keep them gigglin', don't you?" Blair interrupted, as she crossed her arms.

Tobin knew her voice. He didn't even look up at her. He wasn't about to give her any satisfaction. He shook his head, whispered in the young woman's ear. They both rose from their chairs and left.

"You not gonna answer me?"

Before Blair could follow them, Donna snatched Blair by her arm and pulled back. Sabrina and Trisha looked on, in the distance.

"Your friend is showing her ass!" Trisha said, snapping her fingers. "This is what drama dreams are made of!"

"I'd spit on that bitch!" Blair yelled, as the woman scampered across the eatery.

People sitting in the eatery looked at Blair. "What hell y'all looking at?" She snapped. "This ain't y'alls business!"

Tobin made his way across the eatery, flipping Blair his middle finger. Donna held on to Blair by wrapping her arms around her. Blair tussled with Donna and pushed her off. Donna fell back and Blair ran after him.

Donna fell to the floor. "Fuck it, I don't have time for this mess," she made her way to the table where Sabrina and Trisha sat.

"You aren't going to go after her?" Sabrina pleaded.

"Hell no, I don't want to be involved with this mess!" Donna wiped her pants off, sat down and ate.

"I don't think this right!" Sabrina declared, "I'm going to go stop her!"

"Oh no, you're not; that's not any of your business!" Trisha reasoned, "Let her work that out on her own."

Blair caught up to Tobin and his woman friend. She wanted to kick her ass and his ass too.

"So you can't speak?" Blair huffed.

"I can speak; I don't want to speak to you!"

Blair's eyes glazed at the young blonde-haired woman as if a laser was penetrating a steel beam.

"I oughta hit the shit outta this chick, just to wipe that stupid ass smirk off her face!"

"You ain't gonna shit." Tobin shot back.

Tobin knew the only way Blair would back down was to play into her weakness. He wasn't interested in any of the state or local Virginia police showing up because of Blair's fetish for him.

"Look, I'll call you," he said in a calm voice.

"You think it's that easy?" Blair screamed.

As people passed by the mass commotion, Blair knew she needed to end the ruckus before someone caught it with their cell phone camera and posted it to YouTube. She hated that.

"Trust me, I'll call you." Tobin waited for Blair to respond. Then he flashed her, his smile.

"This isn't over!" She said as she walked away.

〜

After the scene at the mall, Sabrina and Trisha hung out at Blair's apartment. Blair made a new drink for everyone to try.

"I need to relax; I almost punched a hole in that girl's face!" Blair bragged as she removed the silver box from under the sofa.

"So why do you think girl was with your boyfriend?" Sabrina asked.

"I have no clue. He and I haven't been getting along lately."

Blair opened the box and sat on the sofa next to Sabrina; she pulled out a joint. She lit it and took a long drag letting the soothing smoke fill up her lungs. Blair coughed, and the smoke blew out like a smoke stack.

"Wanna hit?" Blair offered it to Sabrina and Trisha.

"I'll pass; I'm drug tested at my job." Trisha stated as she waited for Sabrina to decline.

"Sure," Sabrina said as she took the joint and took a hit.

Trisha sat astonished at Sabrina's willingness to try anything. Sabrina coughed out the smoke as Blair laughed. Sabrina took another puff and then passed it back to Blair. Sabrina felt the effect. She leaned back on the sofa and stared at the ceiling then let out a loud chuckle.

"I'm flying," she said.

24

*S*abrina moved the last of her boxes into the elevator. She was glad she hadn't unpacked her stuff from moving her things out of Deacon Byrd's house. She found a nice efficiency apartment near her job close to George Washington University. It was at least a forty-minute ride to work from her parent's house in Bowie to work every morning.

Sabrina hadn't told her parents she was moving. She took the coward's way out by moving out on a Sunday morning when they wouldn't be back for hours. They weren't expecting her at church.

Once she reached the tenth floor, one of the door attendants helped her with the boxes. He was an older man, with silver hair that perfectly matched his soft blue eyes. Sabrina felt guilty for having him help her, but he insisted.

"I saw you having trouble," he said.

"Thank you, I appreciate it so much."

"My name is Ralph, and you're?"

"New to the building, my name is Sabrina."

"I've been working for this company for over fifty years." Ralph continued.

It wasn't to Sabrina's surprise. He looked like he was two steps from having a heart attack as he helped Sabrina move the boxes into the quaint apartment. Sabrina was excited and ready to live on her own. This was a long time coming. The only problem she had was dropping the bomb on Charles and Helen. Sabrina knew Helen wouldn't be happy. Helen had Sabrina under her thumb long enough. It was at Helen's urging that Sabrina marry the deacon. Even if it wasn't for love, it was for the prestige of being related to the Byrds, the most well-known family in Bowie.

Sabrina lifted the last box from the elevator and placed it in the apartment. Ralph stood in the doorway catching his breath. Sabrina dug in her purse and searched for her wallet. She pulled out five dollars she found in a side pocket. She wanted to offer him a little something for all his trouble.

"Please take this," she said as she handed Ralph the money.

Ralph refused. "Oh no miss, you keep it," he said, and he wrapped his soft wrinkled hands around Sabrina's.

Sabrina felt warmth from him. She knew he meant well, and she was happy to have a sweet man to look after her when needed.

As much as she hated it, Sabrina knew it would be difficult to tell her parents she had moved out. She waited at the kitchen table for them to arrive home from church. She grabbed a napkin from the holder on the table to wipe her hands. As she rubbed them together, she heard the car in the driveway. A sharp pain shot through the front of her head. *What is wrong with me? I'm an adult! Get yourself together!*

Helen and Charles entered the kitchen through the back door. Sabrina sat at the table and gave them a pathetic half a smile.

Helen removed her large brim hat from her head as she walked passed Sabrina. Helen gritted and rolled her eyes.

"We didn't see you in church this morning Sabrina," Charles said, as he searched the refrigerator.

Sabrina took a deep breath and let out a long sigh.

"No, I wasn't there. I have something I need to share." Sabrina stood up from the table, and Helen stood stiff at the kitchen breakfast bar with a stone face; Charles lifted from the refrigerator to look at Sabrina.

As Sabrina took a step forward to speak, "Sabrina, your father, and I have been talking, and we think..." Helen said.

"...I've moved out," she blurted before Helen could finish the rest of her sentence.

"Well, I'll be damned!" Helen yelled. "Charles, do something!"

"What do you want me to do Helen?" He yelled back. "The girl is a woman!"

"I knew I wouldn't get any support," Sabrina said, as he left her parents standing dumbfounded and speechless in the kitchen.

It wasn't before long Helen ranted. Her voice carried so far; Sabrina was surprised God didn't call her out and tell her to be quiet.

25

*D*r. Kent knew Blair was the bartender from the Double Sky, but she wasn't sure why Blair would sit on her sofa looking for consultation. Blair didn't strike Dr. Kent as a woman who would seek therapy for any of her problems.

"So, how can I be of help to you?" Dr. Kent sat across from Blair.

"I know you're good at helping people."

"I've helped a few, but how can I help you?" Dr. Kent continued to probe Blair.

Blair walked around the office. She picked up different objects in the room and examined them.

"I think he needs to be trapped."

"I'm sorry, maybe I misunderstood you, did you say trapped, who?"

"Yeah, like a caged animal."

Dr. Kent scribbled a few notes on her notepad. "Blair, you realize we trap animals not people."

"Hey, what the hell are you writing?" Blair snapped, as she approached Dr. Kent.

Dr. Kent twitched in her chair. Blair gave Dr. Kent a crazed and somewhat demonic look.

"I'm just taking notes for my files," Dr. Kent blurted, "these notes are confidential; they are only for me...you know, to remind me of what we talked about, just in case you come back for another session."

"Oh, okay." Blair felt reassured that Dr. Kent wouldn't do anything with her notes.

"If you become a patient of mine, I have to abide by a doctor patient confidentially agreement." Dr. Kent added, to sooth any of Blair's angst.

At that point, Dr. Kent moved behind her desk where she could reach the silent and hidden panic button; just in case.

"He's like my pet, in a way."

Blair continued speaking about Tobin abstractly. Professionally, Dr. Kent thought Blair was teetering on the edge of insanity. She wanted to know more, but Blair's erratic behavior made her nervous.

Dr. Kent nodded her head as her hands shook.

26

Sabrina knew Blair wasn't interested in attending church, but she thought it was a good way to expose Blair to how she grew up. A reversal of sorts.

Sabrina and Blair sat in the rear pews. They were late; sleepy and reeked of Saturday night partying. They still wore the clothing from the night before. The usher let them creep into the last pew while the minister gave his sermon.

"I don't know why I'm here," Blair whispered.

"We all need to repent a little once in a while."

Blair leaned her head on Sabrina's shoulder; the words from Minister Byrd became inaudible as she closed her eyes. Sabrina didn't have the heart to wake Blair as she continued her slumber. For a moment, Sabrina wasn't bothered by Blair's snoring. It was more like a little purr, but at one point, Blair snored so loud, she woke herself up and had to wipe the slobber from her mouth. Sabrina poked her. They giggled. Closer to the front, Helen wanted to shoot Sabrina a few dirty looks, but she sat too far away. Sabrina snickered at the thought of the look on her mother's face.

Priceless.

∽

After the sermon, Sabrina introduced Blair to Cyrus. Out of the corner of her eye, Sabrina saw Helen, Charles, and Trisha on the approach. Cyrus kissed Sabrina on the cheek and gave a nod to the Sloans as he walked away.

"Watch out for this one," he mumbled in passing as he walked to the basement to join the Sunday buffet.

Trisha watched Helen's face. Helen gave a frown while clutching her purse close to her body. Charles and Trisha gave Sabrina a kiss on the cheek as they greeted her. Helen stood still.

"Sabrina, I see you made it to church this Sunday," Charles said.

Sabrina giggled. Helen moved more off to the side, continuing to watch the spectacle.

"Who's your friend here?"

Blair smiled and batted her eyelashes at Charles. Cocking her head, Helen stepped closer to her husband.

"Blair...these are my parents, Charles and Helen Sloan."

"Nice to meet you, Mr. and Mrs. Sloan," Blair said, as she reached out to shake their hands.

Charles extended his hand and gave a hearty laugh, like Santa Claus. Sabrina looked at her father not sure to make of his behavior. Helen grunted at Charles' friendliness.

Blair sensed something familiar about Charles; she felt like she had seen his face before. She couldn't remember where.

"Gotta nice grip there."

Helen shocked by her husband's behavior, turned away, as Minister Byrd approached.

"Sabrina! Nice to see you in church, and nice of you to bring your sleepy friend," Minister Byrd said.

Minister Byrd was always so forgiving. He usually gave a forgiveness sermon at least once a quarter. He wanted to let his members know forgiveness is not for the other person but for himself or herself.

Helen cleared her throat. She grabbed Charles' elbow and tried to pull him away. Helen wanted to make sure Charles didn't get himself wrapped up in any of Sabrina's devil nonsense.

"We should all be getting downstairs for dinner. Nice to meet you Blair, have Sabrina bring you by the house for dinner one evening. Minister, shall we?" Charles asked.

Blair smiled.

Charles guided Helen and the minister to the basement.

"I see why you had to set yourself free." Blair took out a cigarette from her handbag and lit it.

"Come on Blair...not here!" Sabrina turned away from Blair.

---

27

*S*abrina applied a coat of clear lip-gloss on her already shimmery lips. She slightly tweaked her hair and made sure there wasn't any lent on her outfit. She changed from her flats to her heels, gripped the steering wheel and sighed. Girl you look good! Time to go get them!

Sabrina had registered for the speed-dating event weeks ago, even had Trisha's help with an outfit, but since then she had been doing shopping and had a much-improved wardrobe. She didn't tell Blair or anyone but Trisha about the event. She wanted to do this on her own.

Sabrina walked through the lobby of the hotel. In her mind, as she walked, she felt it was in slow motion with the wind blowing through her hair, like a Beyonce video. She was ready to tackle this event head on. As she walked by, two men looked her way. She smiled, waved, and blew them a kiss. She tried not to giggle at her actions. Work it, girl!

~

She entered the lobby of the conference room. A nice young woman, by the name of Matilda, greeted her and checked her off the list.

"Thank you for attending our speed dating event," Matilda said, while handing Sabrina a packet of information. "We have a refreshments room set up down the hall and to your left. We have separated the men from the woman, so your experience will be unique," she stated.

"Thank you." Sabrina gathered her packet and went to the ladies' refreshment room.

As everyone entered the main room, the tables were lined with chairs on each side and numbers on the back of each chair. Everyone was given a number coinciding with a chair. As Sabrina waited to be seated, she noticed Cyrus out of the corner of her eye. Oh shit, what is he doing here?

Cyrus entered the conference room and noticed Sabrina. Her lower lip quivered as she grinned.

Her hair was flowing; her makeup was flawless, as if she came straight from the MAC counter, rocking a short black leather jacket, a low-cut white shirt, tight black jeans, and wedge platform heels. Cyrus couldn't believe his eyes. He hugged her and could get a whiff her of scent. She smelled like a flower shop in full bloom.

"Wow Sabrina, you look great!" He continued to examine her from head to toe.

"I didn't know you speed dated," he said with curiosity, "I never made you to be that girl."

Sabrina raised her eyebrow at Cyrus. "You never know what type of woman a girl is."

Sabrina resented Cyrus being there. She wasn't sure he'd go

back to the church and tell everyone he saw her and how she was dressed. The last thing Sabrina needed was her mother finding out and being confronted once again about her chosen worldly lifestyle.

Cyrus nodded as Sabrina. He knew was cue to keep things moving. He hoped he wouldn't have to sit across from her during the event.

As Sabrina inched away from him, the announcer tapped the microphone at the podium.

"I see we're about to start. Good luck to you tonight." Cyrus said.

"Same to you." Sabrina left him standing there alone.

Sabrina walked out of the conference room with a smile on her face. She felt confident and proud of what she had accomplished during the speed-dating event. Most of the men tried to slip her their number while Matilda wasn't looking. Unlike the speed-dating event, Dr. Kent gave; it was against the rules for participants tell their names or phone numbers. The speed daters were listed by their event number. The event hosts were trying to control every aspect, so the participants would have to pay for the full listing if they wanted to interact with the people, they met that night. The list was about making money; registration was free.

Sabrina wasn't interested in anyone she met. She spoke to at least twenty different men for ten minutes each and thank God; none of them was Cyrus. She could have spoken to more, but called it quits when the last one admitted he'd like to smell the crotch and feet of women's worn pantyhose.

As Sabrina left the conference room, Matilda came running after her.

"Miss Sloan?"

"Yes."

"Here is the list of men who would like to know more about you. I hope you purchase the full list."

The registration clerk handed Sabrina two sheets of paper, not only did it list all twenty men she had spoken to, but it listed an additional fifteen guys she didn't speak with.

Before Matilda could walk away, Sabrina stopped her.

"Is this good?"

"It's the best I've ever seen."

Matilda walked away leaving Sabrina stunned. Sabrina read over the list and shook her head.

I can't believe this!

She tried not to skip out of the conference room wing, but she couldn't help herself and decided to do at least one leap before entering the main lobby.

Sabrina entered the main hotel lobby with the event packet and listing still in her hand; she looked it over one more time as she collided with Tobin. Everything she was holding flew out of her hand and on to the floor.

"Sorry. I'm so sorry," Sabrina said.

"No problem."

Tobin picked the papers up from the floor, and Sabrina snatched them from him.

"You look familiar."

Sabrina gave Tobin a smirk. "I doubt that," she said as she moved passed him while he grabbed her elbow.

"No, I've definitely seen you before; you look different. You were looking for an office building downtown, and I gave you directions."

Sabrina ran her hands through her hair. "I remember that sorta."

"So did you find what you were looking for?"

"I may have."

Tobin rubbed his hand on this chin. He knew Sabrina looked fabulous. Her hair was different, and she dressed differently; but he didn't know what changed the nerdy girl he met on the street, to the woman he was staring at now, but whatever it was; he wanted to know more about her.

Sabrina smiled back.

"Would you like to get coffee?"

Sabrina paused for a moment, "I don't drink coffee."

"No Starbucks?"

"You know; Starbucks sells more than just the liquid crack."

Sabrina scanned Tobin from head to toe. She remembered the smell of the Bvglari from The Danger Ranger. Wearing the same cologne, the scent crept up into her nose like a good Sunday meal. Tobin's clothes fit his body perfectly, the button-down shirt, not tucked in, unbuttoned precisely enough to see his bare chest. His jeans sagged exactly right, worn with a pair of Polo boots.

Sabrina looked deeply into Tobin's light hazel eyes. "I'm not taking you away from any important business am I?"

"No. Am I taking you away from something?"

"Not really."

Sabrina didn't remember him looking this good when they met on the street.

There was something about Tobin that made Sabrina want to float away. His hair was cut short, but on the top were these little locks of black shiny curls.

As he smiled at her, she noticed how perfectly straight and white his teeth were. His smooth skin was mocha brown and not one blemish on this face. And he had the neatest five o'clock shadow.

Sabrina stuffed the paper in her purse. "Just the venti caramel macchiato, right?" She asked with a sly grin.

Tobin and Sabrina ended up at a twenty-four IHOP. They got to the Starbucks too late, it was closed.

An hour later, they were laughing over breakfast and coffee, sharing the stories of their lives.

"My parents were just as strict as yours." Tobin smiled at her. He couldn't stop blushing. This woman really affected him.

Just as nervous and excited, Sabrina said," Strict isn't even the word. So tell me about your music?"

"I play here and there. I like to move around from city to city. Just hoping to a get a permanent band together for that big break."

"Hoping, you better pray…" The word came out before Sabrina knew it.

Tobin just smiled. Maybe he should pray, he thought.

Both smiled at the same time and the conversation continued until sunrise had arrived. Neither one wanted to leave each other.

28

Sabrina hated to leave Tobin, but she needed to get rest. Blair was coming over for dinner with her parents.

Sabrina looked around the table; after the awkward moment at the church, Sabrina didn't know why she invited Blair to dinner as her father had suggested. In addition, she had hoped Trisha cooked instead of Helen.

Sabrina, Blair, Trisha, Charles, and Helen sat around the dining room table. Since they were entertaining a friend of Sabrina's Charles thought, it would be more comfortable to sit at the formal dining room table.

Everyone bowed their heads for grace except for Blair. Helen opened one eye to look at Blair.

"Amen!" Everyone said, except for Blair.

"Let's dig in!" Trisha said.

"The devil is real," Helen mumbled under her breath.

"Sabrina, haven't seen you lately. How has everything been?" Charles asked, "I guess Helen, and I need to come see your new place."

"Everything has been great, Daddy."

"Trisha tells me you met a man," Helen mentioned, keeping an eye on Blair.

Blair looked shocked. Trisha continued to pile food on her plate, trying to ignore the interrogation.

"You didn't tell me you met someone," Blair said.

"Nothing much to say." Sabrina really didn't want everyone to know about Tobin just yet.

"From what I hear, he's really good looking!" Trisha chimed in.

When will she ever learn to shut her mouth?

"Oh, is he now? I can't wait to meet him. What's his name?" Blair asked.

Sabrina felt like she was walking into a trap. Sabrina shifted in her chair. She didn't feel comfortable with Blair's line of questioning. This was her first real relationship. She wanted to take it slow with Tobin, just in case things didn't work out, she could save face.

Trisha could see how uncomfortable Sabrina was becoming. She knew she shouldn't have opened her mouth and spilled the beans.

"Let's change the subject." Trisha interrupted, before Sabrina could say Tobin's name.

"Yes, let's...enough about me. Trisha, how are your classes coming along?"

Sabrina couldn't wait to leave her parent's house. Even though dinner was technically a success because Trisha cooked, she made one fatal mistake of letting her secret out about Tobin.

29

$\mathcal{H}$elen busted into the office of Minister Byrd, just as he was coming out of his personal bathroom. She caught him zippering up his pants. For a moment, their eyes locked, before Helen turned away.

"Lord, forgive me," she whispered to herself.

"Sister Helen, how can I help you today?" Minister Byrd asked without missing a step.

"It's Sabrina. She's just gone mad. She's cut her hair; she moved out. Now, she's got some shady woman friend," Helen said in one breath.

Minister Byrd was the first-person Helen felt she could speak to about Sabrina. Charles wasn't as much help as she thought he would be. He thought it was about time Sabrina exercised freedom.

Helen sat down in front of Minister's Byrd's desk trying to catch her breath. She knew she had said a mouthful, and she wasn't sure how the Minister would take the news of his former daughter-in-law being a harlot.

Minister Byrd sat next to Helen and patted her knee. Helen

loved the reassurance the Minister always provided. She found him to be a kind and gentle soul.

"The woman didn't even say grace at dinner!" Helen fumed.

Minister Byrd sensed Helen's heartache. He took her by the hand and held it firmly. Helen became flustered. She fanned herself with her other hand. This motion by the minister aroused her.

"Sabrina is acting out because of the death of Wallace."

Helen allowed the minister to continue holding her hand; she lost herself in the warmth and comfort of his hands and his words before she snapped back.

"Well, she's met a maaan! I tell you that!" Helen quipped.

"She's in grief."

"I think this is more than grief. She's possessed!" Helen stated as she pounded her fist on his desk.

$\mathcal{I}$t wasn't before long Sabrina and Tobin were spending every day together.

Sabrina stopped coming around the Double Sky, and Blair hadn't heard from Sabrina. She also wondered how Tobin was doing; she hadn't heard from him in a while either. She wanted to call him but wasn't ready to hear the voice of a woman if she answered his phone; or if he answered the phone and told her to go to hell.

Donna tried to convince Blair Tobin wasn't worth the headache, but Blair thought so, she would make Tobin fall in love with her if she didn't do anything else.

Surprised to see Tobin waiting for her with beautiful long stem white roses at her front door, Sabrina smelled them as he moved in closer to her. His eyes twinkled as he pinned her against the wall. Sabrina's legs quivered, and her heart thumped harder and harder as he pressed up against her. He smelled so good behind his ear. He lightly kissed her lips. Sabrina closed her eyes allowing the kiss to linger for a moment. Tobin then gently let his tongue ease between Sabrina's lips into her mouth. His lips were soft, moist, and luscious. He continued to kiss her slowly, allowing his tongue to glide across hers in unison.

Sabrina went underneath Tobin's arms. She took several steps back, pulling away from him. He grabbed her hand and pulled her closer to him. He had a serious look on his face. It was intense. He stared at Sabrina's soft, innocent, and adorable face. Tobin wrapped his arms around her, placing his hands on her lower back.

"I want to make love to you tonight." He whispered in her ear.

Just at the moment, Sabrina heard Donna Summer's song Love to Love You Baby in her head. She didn't know why she wanted to fight the urge. Maybe it was her upbringing and if her mother knew she was having sex before marriage it would kill her. The more she resisted Tobin's advances, the more he wanted her.

They stood in the living room of her apartment. He sucked on her neck. She allowed his soft lips to caress her edge of her chin, down her neck and continuing to her breasts. He unbuttoned each button off her shirt one at a time. She was ready for him to rip her shirt off. She didn't care, but she held back and enjoyed the moment. It took everything in her to be patient as he kissed her again.

"Damn baby, give it to me," she whispered.

Sabrina pulled away from him, unlocking her lips from his and dropping the flowers on the floor. She felt fragile. He gave her a seductive smile then licked his lips. Tobin unbuttoned his shirt, revealing his muscles under his wife beater tee shirt. He then pulled his off his tee shirt, exposing his bare muscular chest and chiseled abs. His skin was a perfect mocha brown, soft and smooth. She loved the fact he only had one tattoo, strategically placed on the upper section of his bicep. Sabrina stared at the upper part of his body.

Sabrina admired Tobin's body. Sabrina wasn't sure what she was about to get into, but whatever it was; the thought of it made her moist. Tobin stepped towards Sabrina; Sabrina stepped back into the bedroom room. Tobin followed. He came within inches of Sabrina's lips. She gazed into his light hazel eyes. His eyes showed sensitivity, warmth, and - horniness.

Tobin picked Sabrina up; she wrapped her legs around his body. They continued to kiss deeply, letting their tongues dance in each other's mouths. Then he kicked the bedroom door shut.

Sabrina lay next to Tobin as he slept. She looked out the window from her bed and saw nighttime had fallen. The excitement of making love to him played in her mind. She caressed her arm the way he did. She glided her hand up her arm softly, feeling the goose bumps rise on her skin. The thought of him sleeping soundly next her, made her anxious and aroused. She wanted him to wake up and make love to her all over again.

Sabrina finally forced herself to sleep. When she awakened, Tobin held her close. It was the motion of him playing in her hair that woke her up. He kissed her earlobe, and then kissed her cheek, making his way to her lips.

Sabrina lay still in the bed with her eyes closed. The thought of him kissing her in the morning with morning breath mortified her.

"Wake up, sleepy head," he said.

Sabrina stirred, and she slowly opened her eyes.

I can't believe he is here.

She smiled at him as he leaned in sneaking in another kiss.

"Hey you."

"Hey you too."

Tobin kissed her nose instead and pulled her closer just as the phone rang. Sabrina reached for the phone. He pulled her arm back. They kissed again. He tried to wrestle the phone away from her. The phone continued to ring. He tickled her when she answered it.

"Hel-lo, hello." Answering the phone with a laugh.

Tobin kissed Sabrina on the neck. She giggled more.

The person on the other end continued to speak. Tobin got on top of Sabrina. He put her nipples in his mouth and sucked on her breasts. Sabrina's legs opened, ready to receive what he was about to give. Tobin rubbed up and down her; he wanted to be inside of her.

"Hey. Let me call you back." She could barely speak.

Sabrina dropping the phone on the floor not even sure if the phone hung up.

Tobin made love to her again.

Depressed and feeling alone, Blair hung up the phone from Sabrina. She lay in the bed thinking about all the fun Sabrina must have been having with her new man. The thought of Sabrina having a man, made Blair furious with rage and jealousy. She didn't think it was fair that an out of place nerdy church chick was being loved down royally while she yearned for Tobin.

Blair called Tobin, hoping he'd answer. She thought she could sweet talk him into coming over, just for old time's sake. What's a little thump in the bed between former roommates, almost serious lovers, she wondered? When she called, his phone went straight to voice mail. She hung up before she heard the beep.

Sabrina wanted to share the news about Tobin with someone. She wanted to share it with the world if she could. She hadn't spoken to Dr. Kent since that day she snooped in the patient files, but she sat in Dr. Kent's office.

"I met a man."

"Really? Tell me about him."

"He's wonderful. He's a musician. He's from Ohio, the oldest of eight, has a body built like Adonis and treats me like a queen. He reminds of Dwayne 'The Rock' Johnson."

"Hmmm, that sounds sexy. You're a lucky girl; I'm glad to hear this. You definitely have a glow."

Tobin was the sexiest man Sabrina has ever been within her life. She cherished the moments they spent together. He was always a complete gentleman. Every time, they went out, he paid. It was as if God handpicked him for her; she was blessed.

Sabrina twirled her hair. "I feel WONDERFUL!" She shouted, and then she covered her face with her hands while she laughed.

Sabrina was still a God-fearing woman at heart, even through her transformation; she felt she was still a good person.

"I credit you, Dr. Kent for my relationship with Tobin."

"Me?"

"It was because of you, I'm here, so I feel the need to apologize."

"Apologize?" Dr. Kent said bewildered.

Sabrina believed in karma. Now that happiness found her with Tobin, she didn't want God to yank it away by keeping this secret from Dr. Kent.

"Yes. I lied to you."

"About what?" She said confused.

Dr. Kent went back through her mind. She wasn't sure what Sabrina was trying to say. Sabrina couldn't have known about Wallace.

Sabrina took a deep breath. "I snooped through your files. I was looking for evidence of Deacon Byrd being your patient." Sabrina sighed with relief.

"You did what?"

Dr. Kent didn't know what to think of Sabrina's admission. She could have jumped on her about snooping in her old files, but she had suspected Sabrina had snooped but wasn't ready to admit to it. Dr. Kent knew Sabrina's heart; she meant well, and that she had longed for answers about Wallace, but she didn't condone lying.

Sabrina looked at Dr. Kent, ready for the tongue-lashing.

"I apologize." Sabrina hung her head. She only hoped Dr. Kent was a forgiving woman.

It seemed like an eternity for Dr. Kent to speak.

Deep inside, Dr. Kent wanted to tell Sabrina about her affair with Wallace, but she knew admission would open an assortment of questions, and questions can lead to problems, much greater than Sabrina snooping into her file cabinet. For now, it was best for Sabrina to think she was the only one at fault.

"I'm glad you came clean, Sabrina. I forgive you."

Sabrina met Tobin at Lake Waterford Park after her appointment with Dr. Kent. The sun hadn't quite set yet, but the warm weather and the breeze that blew threw her hair made her feel giddy. Tobin had given Sabrina a map of where she was to meet him in the park. Lake Waterford Park reminded her of Central Park, not as big, but it had a beautiful two-mile wide lake in the middle where people liked to jog around it.

Tobin set up a blanket under a large tree. From the distance, he could see the lake as the rays from the sun reflected on to the water. Then Sabrina glimpsed Tobin. He stood taller then normal from a distance. She ran to him, and he playfully he ran away. She chased him, laughing, and smiling at the silliness of playing tag. Once she got him, she tackled him down on the ground. They rolled around on the grass. He kissed her. Then she broke free from him and took off running again. Tobin chased her.

31

*B*usier than as usual for the midday rush, Blair wiped down the bar and served drinks; she didn't see Cyrus enter the bar, but he saw her. Cyrus sat in the last chair on the end. He watched as Blair moved about fixing drinks. He liked the way her low-rise jeans grabbed the roundness of her ass. It was as if her jeans were painted onto her body, they were so formfitting.

The last time Cyrus saw Blair was at the church. He couldn't help admiring her body then, and he thought he'd take another peek now. He was on the prowl for a hit.

Blair wasn't feeling the scene in the Double Sky. She couldn't get her mind off of Tobin. She went back in her mind, thinking of how she could have made things better with him. She used her hard exterior to protect herself from rejection and abandonment, something she continually experienced most of her life. In the end, he rejected and abandoned her, anyway.

"What would you like?" Blair asked, not recognizing Cyrus.

"Just water."

Blair ignored Cyrus. "Look you can buy water at the seven

eleven down the street. We don't serve 'just water'," she said annoyed.

Blair cleaned off the bar. She didn't even attempt to get Cyrus the water he tried to order.

"Well, then can I have just you?" he asked.

"No, this corny ass Negro didn't! Get the hell outta here before I call security," she screeched at Cyrus. "Weirdo."

Dr. Kent sat behind her desk and watched Blair lying on the sofa. Blair seemed entranced by the smoothness of her skin as she laid-back and rubbed her arms from the tip of her fingers to edge of her armpit.

"I think he has a girlfriend."

"And why do you think he has a girlfriend?"

"I can just feel it."

"I think it's time you let this obsession go Blair. This isn't healthy. If he does have a girlfriend, you need to let it go. He's moved on. Why can't you?"

Blair snapped out of her daze of rubbing her arms and grabbed the letter opener from Dr. Kent's desk. She leaned over the desk and stuck it in her face.

"Obsession? Fuck that! I will never let Tobin go!" Blair hollered. "Ain't this some shit? You're supposed to help me, and your best advice is to tell me to let it go? You crazy. I ain't letting shit go!"

Dr. Kent froze. She tried to slide her hand to the panic button under her desk. Her hand trembled. Blair threw the letter opener down on the desk.

Dr. Kent managed to press the panic button under her desk, but she wasn't sure what to make of Blair being obsessed with this phantom man. Dr. Kent wanted to question Blair more about it, but she wasn't sure if this was the right time. She wanted her to calm down.

Blair slouched back on to the sofa as a heavyset security guard bum rushed the door.

"Is everything all right here? We got a buzz," he panted.

"I must have accidentally hit the button by mistake." Dr. Kent placed the letter opener into her desk drawer.

Dr. Kent concluded her session with Blair without asking Blair any questions or giving her any more advice. She did manage to learn about Donna, Blair's best friend. Dr. Kent decided she needed to visit Donna to gather more information on Blair's mental state.

32

_S_urprised, Tobin agreed to come to church; Sabrina and Tobin sat next to Charles and Helen during the Sunday morning sermon. Despite her newfound freedom, Sabrina still felt the need to keep in the good graces of God as much as she could. She didn't attend church every Sunday, but she tried to attend at least twice a month.

Tobin placed his arm around Sabrina's shoulder; with Helen constantly looking over her own to make sure there wasn't any funny business going on.

Helen thought Tobin was a nice-looking young man, but she knew little about his background. Sabrina wouldn't tell anyone much about him. Did she have something to hide? Helen specifically wondered about his religiousness. She figured he had to be God fearing coming from Ohio. Who comes from Ohio and isn't Godly?

Out, the side of her eye, Helen caught some of the members from the first family, attempting to get a look at Sabrina and Tobin from across the aisle. Helen rolled her eyes and frowned. It was so disappointing that Deacon Byrd died, not to mention, Sabrina's behavior since. The first family didn't know what to make of it all. Helen feared they would kick them out of the church for not being good God-fearing people. Helen knew; Sabrina's actions were not a decent look in the eyes of the first family or the church elders.

Sabrina glanced at her mother looking at the first family. She knew Helen was disappointed as to how everything panned out; but with the death of the deacon, this was her opportunity to live her life as she wanted. Sabrina didn't pay any attention to the many looks, she and Tobin received. She wasn't sure if they were looking at him because he was good looking, or they were just being nosey. It was probably both. She was with a fine ass man and it must have driven some of the single women crazy, how she of all people could snag him. Tobin didn't notice the looks or the stares. He smiled at Sabrina and kissed her on her cheek. He was happy to be in her space. At the sight of the kiss, one church elder turned her head in disgust. Helen grimaced, clutched her purse, and shook her head. How dare Sabrina flaunt her affair for all to see? Helen figured she'd deal with Sabrina's disrespectful behavior later. While the choir sung, Minister Byrd took mental notes of Sabrina's conduct.

Sabrina clapped her hands to the music.

On the other side of the aisle sat Dr. Kent. Despite Wallace being dead, Dr. Kent decided she'd continue to go to church. She missed Wallace a lot, and even though she wasn't the most religious woman in the world, going to the church helped her feel connected to him. She was even surprised at herself for taking this leap.

She knew how the people whispered and talked about her behind her back. As a psychologist, the contradiction of actions and the word of God were baffling to her. Were Christians accepting or not? Was forgiveness available for all or just those who attend church every Sunday? What gave the church elders the right to judge?

Dr. Kent enjoyed the sermon; Minister Byrd spoke of forgiveness. It was something Dr. Kent needed to hear. It was something she thought everyone needed to hear. There seemed to be a lack of it floating around in the air within the church.

In spite of all the negativity, Dr. Kent had decided she would come back to the church more often; regardless of the older members' dirty looks.

As Dr. Kent left the church, she was confronted by Helen.

"Excuse me!" Helen screamed out to Dr. Kent's back.

Dr. Kent turned around to find a frustrated Helen Sloan's piercing eyes. If Dr. Kent didn't know any better, she thought she saw fire glazing up from Helen's soul into her eyeballs.

"Mrs. Sloan, are you okay?"

Helen looked around for other church members. She wouldn't dare be caught speaking to this spectacle of a woman, but this was for Sabrina's sake, not her own.

"I shouldn't be talking to you, but..."

"But here you stand," Dr. Kent tried not to be too bold, but she was coming close to the edge of telling everyone about their hypocrisy.

Helen held her head up. She wouldn't let Dr. Kent speak to her any kind of way. She gave the doctor a penetrating stare, searching for her soul within her eyes.

"I know Sabrina has come to see you. Whatever 'spell' you have on her. I've prayed to God that you'd let her go. God is stronger than the devil, don't you EVER forget that." Helen was resounding. Her voice was deep and strong. She was throwing the gauntlet down on Dr. Kent.

Dr. Kent laughed. It sounded evil, but Dr. Kent only toyed with Helen's emotions.

"Helen, if I may call you that..."

"...you may not!" Helen roared.

"I have no spell on Sabrina. Sabrina needed to experience life. She needed to enjoy life more. You were holding her back. She's having what we normal people call FUN," Dr. Kent walked away from Helen uninterested in any further conversation. She didn't want any scenes by the church.

Helen remained behind; standing steadfast in her place. She didn't move or speak. The words wouldn't release themselves from her mind to her mouth. She was speechless. Christian or not, Helen had a few choice words she would have liked to have said, but it was the Lord's work she stood motionless.

The sun fell over the horizon. The lights to the rides at the carnival lit up at dusk. More and more people entered on to the Maryland State Fairgrounds; the carnival music played, and the kids ran wildly looking to be the first ones on the rides. Sabrina remembered going to the carnival with her parents when she was younger. It was always the best of times, but as she and Trisha grew older, and her parents seem to get more aliments; they stopped going to the carnival.

Tobin took Sabrina's hand and led her to the Ferris wheel. Sabrina hated the Ferris wheel. It was high, looked unsafe, and shook as it went around. She always wondered how the carnival mechanics put it together from town to town and not forget to put all the screws in place.

As Sabrina and Tobin reached the top, the Ferris wheel stopped. They were the only ones on the wheel. Tobin slipped the kid working the wheel an additional ten bucks to stop it at the top for an extra five minutes.

Sabrina glanced over the skyline, overlooking Timonium,

trying to see as far as she could. "I never thought my life could be like this."

"Me either." Tobin agreed.

Sabrina looked over at Tobin. His eyes were gleaming; Sabrina wanted to lean over and kiss him, but she enjoyed staring at his loving angelic like face. "You've just changed my life," she said.

"You've changed mine, too, and that's why I love you," he said, as the Ferris wheel descended, and he pulled her closer.

He loves me.

This was the first-time Tobin ever told any woman he loved her and truly meant it.

Sabrina worked in her cubicle, singing a love song she was listening to from her iPod, as the deliveryman gave her flowers over her shoulder. Sabrina jumped at the sight of the flowers. There were a dozen long stem roses mixed with red, white, and yellow. They came in a heavy crystal vase. Sabrina could tell whoever gave her the flowers; they spent a lot of money.

"For me?" Sabrina felt a pit in her stomach. It was so exciting to get flowers at work. Everyone wondered whom the flowers were from, but Sabrina never let on. She never wanted to mix her job with her personal life. Not like, she did when she was working at the church.

"Now are they from you?" She asked the deliveryman.

Sabrina was used to seeing the flower deliveryman. Every other week the married woman next to her cubicle was getting flowers. Her husband was always apologizing for something. One day the woman told Sabrina, she only liked to make a fuss at her husband, so he'd send the flowers. It made her feel special.

"I wish they were, but not this time love," he stated in his thick Jamaican accent.

She read the CARD attached: DINNER TONIGHT. TOBIN. Sabrina shrieked in excitement.

Later that evening, Sabrina took all the clothes out of her closet looking for something to wear. She called in reinforcement, and Trisha came over after her last class. Sabrina wanted to look special for Tobin that evening, and she didn't want him to see anything she had previously worn together. She figured even if is the same pair of pants he wouldn't notice because the shirt would make it look like it was new. Trisha knew better and brought a few items from her closet and some accessories. Her mindset was that accessories could make or break an outfit.

Trisha sat on the bed. Sabrina held up a black skirt, then a blue skirt.

"How do you think this one looks? Tobin loves to see me in black."

"That's cute. But I like the navy one better."

Sabrina switched the skirts back and forth while looking in the mirror. She matched them up with different blouses and shirts with Trisha's accessories.

"I think you should stop hanging with Blair," Trisha said.

"Why?" Sabrina looked in the mirror; she held up a hot pink shirt to the black skirt.

"Her elevator stops short. It's like it doesn't even get off the ground floor."

Sabrina stopped what she's doing and sat next to Trisha on the bed, "Blair is a weed smoker. You know how they are."

"Just be careful. That trick has a treat for you. I know what I'm talking about."

Trisha jumped off the bed; she grabbed the light-blue Jones New York sleeveless V-neck blouse and matched it together with the navy blue skirt she got from Macy's - on sale - with crystal blue baubles she copped from Nordstrom's one day.

Sabrina sighed; yet again Trisha hooked up another fabulous outfit.

"One day, I'm going to get the hang of this!"

Tobin drove Sabrina to one of the best restaurants in town, Tony and Joes, in Georgetown, off the small pier. The stars were clear in the night sky. Usually, it was hard to see the stars up in the sky due to the bright lights of the city. Tonight, was different; the stars sparkled high above them as they walked in. Tobin made reservations a few days prior; getting a good table at this hot spot usually took weeks, but someone he worked with knew the head host, and he could squeeze them in for an eight o'clock reservation. The host escorted them to small room with a booth and a privacy curtain next to a large pane glass window overlooking the Potomac River. The booth was cozy and secluded. Tobin sat close to Sabrina.

"You're beautiful," he remarked.

Sabrina blushed as he kissed her on her neck. She loved it when he kissed her on the inside part of her neck. It was her hot spot, and it made her horny.

Damn, can you do that again? Sabrina let out a low tone moaned.

"Sabrina, there is something I want to say to you."

"Is everything okay?" Sabrina replied, as she raised her eyebrow.

Tobin exhaled; he wasn't sure how too, he wanted to come out and say what he had to say, "I love you; you know that."

"Tobin, you're scaring me, is something wrong?"

Sabrina had never seen Tobin look so serious. He looked as if his whole world depended on what he had to say.

"That's just it; everything is so right, so right I want us to live together."

Sabrina put her hands over her mouth. The words wouldn't come out. Tobin sat in silence not sure what to think about Sabrina's reaction.

"Really?" She responded after her long pause.

Tobin kissed Sabrina. "Yes, really. I don't want any other woman. You're everything. I want to share my life with you."

Sabrina hugged Tobin. She was unsure if this was the right move. She loved Tobin, but she hadn't explored what life offered fully. What if he's not the one? "You don't think we're moving too fast?"

"It's not fast enough."

"Okay. Okay, let's do it then." Sabrina said in a whisper.

Tobin hugged Sabrina as tight as he could. This was a brand new start.

Blair listened to sad love songs as she danced around the room with her invisible partner - the air. She imagined she was in the arms of Tobin. In between songs, she smoked a joint and took a few sips of a drink she made up. She stared at her cell phone. She hoped Tobin would call her to say hi or see about a few of his belongings she took, in hopes he'd come looking for them. He never did.

Just as Blair continued with her thoughts of Tobin, there was a knock at the front door. She rushed to the door. Before she opened it, she fixed her clothes and pulled her hair into a ponytail. She struck a pose and then opened the door - wide.

"Damn girl, what is up with you? You know Tobin is ghost."
Donna let herself in.

That's the last thing Blair needed was the extra haggling from
Donna about Tobin being gone. Blair could see and feel that
Tobin was ghost, and she didn't need it reconfirmed.

"Even that pathetic church chick, Sabrina has a man!"

The thought of Sabrina enjoying her life with this mystery
man drove Blair even more insane. She never expected Sabrina to
find a man this soon. She wasn't finished converting her from a
Saint to a sinner.

"Girl, get dressed...we're going out tonight!" Donna said.

"I'm not going any damn where. This is my night off, and I'm
chillin'."

"Oh, yes we are! I'm tired of you trippin' around this camp.
There are more men out there, better men than Tobin." Donna
pushed Blair into the bedroom.

Mookie's Jazz Club was a little-known joint in Old Town
Alexandria. It was around for years, launching the many careers of
up-and-coming jazz artists. On Sunday nights, Mookie liked to
feature jazz bands that made it to the big time like Kenny G or
Boney James. The club looked like a hole in the wall from the
outside, but once inside, there was a nice size stage with a dance
floor, small round tables with chairs that weren't very comfortable.
In the back, lounge chairs and sofas for those wanted to be more
interactive with discussion, but still wanted to hear the music as a
backdrop.

Donna had been to Mookie's twice before, and she thought it
would be nice for Blair to experience something different. She
decided Blair needed culture; it wasn't always about hip-hop and
hanging out with the young folk like the crowd at the Double Sky.

They found a table in the back to sit and enjoy the sounds of Manifest, the newest nu soul band to hit the scene.

"Donna," Blair whined, "this is not my kind of hang out."

"You need something different."

Donna moved to the tunes of the live band. She watched the people dancing on the dance floor, "I'd love to know how to dance like that."

"I need a puff," Blair said.

"Damn already? We got here. Relax, I'll order you another drink."

"Whatever." Blair headed off to the ladies' room.

Just as Blair disappeared into the restroom, Tobin and Sabrina entered the club. Tobin chose a table close to the front, but off in a cozy corner, and within eyesight of Donna and Blair's table.

Tobin performed at Mookie's many times. He and Mookie had become friends and wasn't anything for him to get a table, even with a standing room only crowd.

As Tobin and Sabrina took a seat, a man asked Donna to dance. She accepted and followed the tall older gentleman to the dance floor. From where Donna stood, she saw Tobin and Sabrina snuggling at their cozy table.

Donna knew if Blair saw Tobin, she'd have a fit, but if she saw Tobin with Sabrina, there would be blood drawn.

Donna tried to dance her way off the dance floor to warn Blair. She didn't know what she would tell her, but the last thing she wanted to see was Blair make a scene in Mookie's. The more Donna tried to dance away from the man, the more he pulled her close. Donna was trapped.

Sabrina kissed Tobin as she left the table. She walked toward the restroom.

There was no stopping the inevitable.

Sabrina walked through the crowded club, but she didn't see Donna, but Donna saw her.

Inside the bathroom stall, Blair took small puffs of a broken off cigarette she had stashed in her wallet. She tried to smoke it quickly so no one who entered the bathroom could smell it. Just as she flushed the remains of the cigarette in the toilet, Sabrina and another woman entered the restroom.

"Uh! It stinks in here," Sabrina said.

"You're right. It smells like someone has been smoking in here," the other woman said.

"Smells just like this cigarette I know this girl smokes. It is God-awful. She doesn't even know how bad she stinks," Sabrina said.

Blair listened from the stall. She didn't make a sound or move, but she knew was Sabrina's voice. Her voice was unmistakable.

"But I know it can't be her," Sabrina continued, "she wouldn't be caught dead in an establishment like this; she's too ghetto." Sabrina stood in the mirror and fixed her hair and makeup.

Who the fuck does this do-gooder church chick calling ghetto? Blair screamed in her head. I'll show that bitch ghetto!

"Well, it's never like this. I'm going to let Mookie know," the woman said.

"This is my first time here. It was my boyfriend's suggestion."

Blair was just about to jump out on Sabrina when she heard her mention her boyfriend. She tried to peep through the crack of the stall door. She heard Sabrina, and the woman leave. She waited for a moment before coming out of the stall. Blair knew this was an opportunity to get a good look at Sabrina's boyfriend and blast her for the ghetto comment.

Blair caught up with Donna on the crowded dance floor. "I think I heard Sabrina's voice in the bathroom."

Donna continued to dance. "No way, you must be hearing things," Donna excused herself from the gentleman; he finally let her go.

Donna walked in the opposite direction of Sabrina and Tobin. The other way was quicker, but they would've had to passed Sabrina and Tobin.

"Don't be silly. I'm about to leave with my dancing dude. He's going to take me home," Donna sat down at the table. "We can leave together."

Blair gulped down the rest of her drink. "I'm telling you, Sabrina is here. I'm going to take a walk around the club."

It was hard for Blair to maneuver around with so many people in the club. She finally gave up and left with Donna and the older man.

Sabrina and Trisha walked around the Target. Target was one of Sabrina's most favorite stores, and it was easy for her to spend over her budget every time she went. Today, she looked around at the house wares area.

"What's up with you sis? You're glowing."

Sabrina stood in the middle of the aisle looking at towels; she picked up a brown towel and held it up for Trisha.

"It's a brown towel. What? Tobin wants a brown towel?" Trisha asked.

Sabrina couldn't contain her excitement any longer. "He wants us to live together!" Sabrina shouted aloud before covering her mouth.

"Are you serious?" Trisha had to pause for second or two. "That's a big step."

"I know, but it feels right."

Sabrina grabbed a few of the dark towels and washcloths. The thought of she and Tobin living together made her feel good about her future.

"I'm happy for you sis." Trisha stated.

Sabrina didn't seem to think Trisha was being genuine. She brushed it off, just as long as she was happy, it didn't matter what Trisha thought.

---

33

*T*obin stood along the crowded sidewalk trying not to bump into any of the K Street lobbyist professionals leaving work for the day. He stood off to the side near the entrance to Sabrina's office building. He thought about what Sabrina meant to him, and he was happy she was in his life. He never thought Blair was a bad person; he wasn't attracted to her in the way she wanted him to be. Fully aware of the mistakes he made by having a sexual relationship with Blair, he told her repeatedly; they were both lonely and needed to let off some steam. If Blair didn't get it that was her problem.

As Tobin reminisced, he didn't see Blair walking to Sabrina's building from the opposite side of the street.

Blair hadn't seen Sabrina in a while and decided she'd surprise her; she had an appointment that wasn't far from Sabrina's job and the pop up gave Blair the perfect excuse to probe Sabrina more about her mystery boyfriend. She also wanted to get her back for that night at the club because she was sure it was Sabrina. The one person she didn't expect to see was Tobin. Viewing him from across the street, she wondered did he know Sabrina or was he waiting for someone else? She hung back to let the scene unfold; she ducked behind a minivan.

Moments later, Blair peeped around the minivan to see Tobin kissing Sabrina. Shocked, a large knot swelled in her gut. Her initial reaction was to confront them but making a scene wouldn't get her the answers she needed. All it would do was push Tobin closer to Sabrina and Blair would look more desperate than she already appeared. Instead, she followed them back to Sabrina's apartment.

Two days later Blair invited Sabrina over to the Double Sky. She wanted to find out all she could about Tobin.

When Sabrina received Blair's invite, she wasn't interested in going out, but since Tobin had to work late, Sabrina decided it was something to do to get out of the house until he came over later.

Sabrina sat at the bar and swayed to the music. The crowd was light, and Sabrina enjoyed one of Blair's concoctions.

"I need to get home," Sabrina said.

Blair wiped the bar off and poured drinks out, cleaning up the bar before the late crowd trickled in.

"You just got here. So, tell me about this great guy you're seeing. He's got all your time these days." Blair stopped what she was doing and paid close attention to every word, Sabrina had to say.

Sabrina blushed as she thought about Tobin. Tobin was the perfect man. She wanted to tell Blair just enough, but not too much.

"Nothing much to say, except he's great looking." Sabrina stopped herself short before saying, "He's great in bed."

Blair frowned for a moment. She knew that; tell her something she didn't know. Blair wanted more details. She wanted to know how they met, the things he has said to her, and how serious it was.

"Are you okay?" Sabrina asked.

"I'm fine."

Blair turned her back and bit her lip. It took everything within her to hold herself together. She wanted to break out a can whip ass on Sabrina, but she knew it wasn't Sabrina's fault - partly. Sabrina didn't know Blair and Tobin were roommates who occasionally slept together. But that didn't stop Blair from feeling rejected. Blair wanted to lash out at anyone who captured Tobin's heart, including Sabrina. It didn't matter they were supposed to be friends. This was about a man, her man.

"He pays for everything. He sends me flowers. He's there when I get off work to take me home," Sabrina continued.

Blair kept her back turned away from Sabrina. Sabrina knew she was digging deep into Blair's mind. She couldn't help herself. Since Sabrina met Blair, Blair acted as if she was better than her, especially, when it came to men. This was Sabrina's opportunity to rub it in some. She was enjoying herself.

Blair took a deep breath and exhaled before turning around to face her arch rival.

"Sounds like a real gentleman," Blair replied, as her hands shook. Blair took a deep breath. The tension was rising within her.

"He is. That's why I must leave. He's probably at my place worried about me. He's just so perfect." Sabrina added.

Sabrina gathered her things, paid for her drink, and began to leave when Blair stopped her.

"So you all live together?"

"Most of his stuff is at my place, but we are working on it." Sabrina paused for a moment; she looked Blair in her eyes.

"Maybe we will get married one day and have babies who look just like him."

The words that came out of Sabrina's mouth, Blair heard them in slow motion. Marriage and babies lingered in her mind like an omen. Blair wouldn't allow Sabrina to marry Tobin.

Blair came from behind the bar giving Sabrina a tight hug, patting her on the shoulder.

Game on bitch! Blair thought.

Sabrina left wondering why Blair gave her such a tight hug. She had never seen Blair so emotional about anything before.

When Sabrina arrived home, Tobin was there, looking out the window as the sunset across the Washington, DC horizon. As she walked to him, putting her hand out for him to take, he did, and pulled her close. They both looked out the window at the beauty of the orange sun.

"I love you," Tobin whispered into Sabrina's ear.

Sabrina paused for moment; hearing those words from someone who really meant them made her eyes fill with tears.

"I love you."

They continued to stare at the sunset as it disappeared behind the buildings.

Blair paced behind the bar. She tapped her hand on the phone; then made a phone call.

Tobin's phone went straight to voicemail.

"Tobin, this is Blair. You left something at my apartment. You can pick it up at the Double Sky tomorrow night around seven."

Blair hung up the phone. She dialed another number.

Sabrina's phone went straight to voicemail.

"Sabrina, I need to talk to you. Come by the Double Sky tomorrow night around seven."

Blair hung up. She looked at herself in the mirror behind the liquor shelves, somewhat pleased with herself.

"It's on!" She said to herself.

34

_C_harles sat at the patio table in the backyard, reading his daily newspaper. Helen sat across from him in a lounge chair drinking her lemonade. It was a nice day to lounge around. Helen tried to get her mind off Sabrina. She was very concerned; Sabrina didn't call as much as she used to, and it was hard for Helen to let go. Helen also despised the fact; Charles didn't seem worried.

Trisha entered the backyard covered in her bathrobe. She dropped her belongings next her mother, and she plopped down next to her father at the table under the umbrella.

"We should invite Sabrina and her friend over for dinner," Trisha mentioned.

"Not that whore again," Helen interrupted.

Charles looked at Helen over the rim of his newspaper as he usually did. He was tiring of Helen's nonsense.

"Well, she is a whore. She's the one that's corrupting Sabrina's mind. Sabrina doesn't even come to church anymore and when she does she brings these shady characters with her!" Helen continued.

"Helen let it go. At one point, you thought it was Dr. Kent, who was corrupting Sabrina's mind." Charles said, nonchalantly.

Trisha ignored Helen and grabbed a piece of the newspaper on the table. She made herself a fan.

"Sabrina is dating a nice guy. They seem serious. I think we need to know more about him. That's all I'm saying." Trisha added.

"We need to stay out of Sabrina's life," Charles concluded, without looking up from his paper.

"This is when she needs us the most, Charles," Helen insisted.

"She's fine."

Trisha slipped off her bathrobe. She revealed a skimpy string bikini.

Helen almost fainted at the sight of it. "What in the tarnation do you have on young lady?" Helen asked. Helen was relived; they were only in their backyard and not at the beach.

"Not much!" Trisha said as she pulled the other lounge chair out to tan.

35

----

*B*lair was serving drinks to the customers at the bar when Sabrina arrived at the Double Sky, she found a nice cozy seat near the end of the bar. Sabrina didn't want to come, but in the message she received from Blair it sounded like she needed to tell her something, so she came. Whatever Blair had to tell her, she prayed it was quick; she couldn't wait to get home to Tobin.

"WHAT'S UP?" Blair yelled over the music and crowd noise in the bar.

Blair was feeling especially good. She knew Sabrina would find out about Tobin and her; thinking Tobin would eventually wise up and come running back to her.

"What do you have to tell me? I have to get home!"

"Just wait." Blair paused.

Blair looked at her watch, it was ten minutes after seven, and Tobin still hadn't arrived yet. She wouldn't be able to keep Sabrina at the bar longer than seven thirty.

Placing a Bully in front her, Sabrina swayed to the music. Blair figured Sabrina would need it...not to drink, but to throw it in Tobin's face when she learned the truth.

Five more minutes passed by before Tobin entered the bar. It seemed like an eternity to Blair. When Blair saw, Tobin, and she motioned to him to come closer to Sabrina; as he moved in, he looked surprised to see her. Hanging back in the corner, Blair watched their faces before coming back over.

"What are you doing here?" He questioned Sabrina.

"What do you mean?"

"Why are you here?" He yelled.

Sabrina had never seen Tobin this agitated. He had never yelled at her before, but he was not happy about her sitting at the bar within range of Blair.

"I came to see Blair."

Blair moved in closer to Sabrina and Tobin.

"Sabrina, I see you've met my boyfriend. We're back together now." Blair's mouth smiled as wide as the ocean, with a speck of the devil shining through. Tobin could sense Blair's slyness; and it took everything within him not hit her across the bar.

"YOUR WHAT?" Sabrina hollered.

Tobin slammed his hand on the bar. "Blair cut it!" Tobin shouted.

"Tobin, are you Blair's boyfriend?" Sabrina demanded.

"Sabrina...let me explain!" Tobin said.

Sabrina looked at Tobin, not sure what to think.

Sabrina gathered her things and ran out the bar.

Blair stood off to the side and laughed. "Pathetic!" Blair shouted out as she couldn't stop laughing when Tobin chased after Sabrina.

Outside the bar, Sabrina felt sick. She felt the weight of the world on her shoulders; she gasped for air. The street and stoplights blurred and streaked through her tears.

Tobin grabbed Sabrina; he wanted to explain everything to her. Sabrina shoved him off.

"You didn't tell me you had a girlfriend!" Sabrina screamed.

"Blair and I were never together; she was never my girlfriend!"

It wasn't before long when Blair appeared between Sabrina and Tobin. Sabrina continued to catch her breath through her hysterical sobbing.

"We lived together! We slept together!" Blair shouted and stood close to Sabrina. "Say it ain't true?" Blair dared Tobin.

What could Tobin say? Was it not true, even if distorted?

"Don't backtrack now!" Blair continued.

"Blair, you're such a bitch!"

Out of Sabrina's view, Blair taunted Tobin by making faces.

Tobin stepped to Sabrina. He tried to touch her, but Sabrina's wasn't interested.

"Don't touch me!" She wailed out. "Never touch me again!"

"Sabrina, we need to talk." Tobin tried to remain calm. "Let's go home."

Sabrina looked away from Tobin. "I don't want to hear what you have to say," she said, "I don't want to ever see you again. Get your shit outta my house!"

Sabrina ran down the street to her car, never looking back.

Blair smiled at Tobin. "That will teach your ass a lesson about double crossing me!" Blair adding her two cents in for good measure.

"Sabrina! Wait up!" Blair called behind Sabrina.

Tobin wanted to chase Sabrina, but he knew with Blair right in the mix it would be impossible to get things straight. He let her go. He knew she needed time. Time to think. Time to process and absorb it all. In the meantime, he wanted to crush Blair like can of soda.

He decided he'd go over to her apartment the next morning.

The next morning Tobin went to Sabrina's to explain, he didn't want to use his key. He knocked on the door. There was no answer. He waited for her for thirty minutes before letting himself in. She wasn't there.

Sabrina finally went back to her apartment after a few days of hanging out with Trisha. Her parents said little while she was there, they were just happy to have her in the house again.

She noticed Tobin had come by and removed his things and left the key on her bedroom nightstand.

Just a few days ago, Tobin was here with her marveling at the sunset, today he was gone. She felt alone. The phone rang; Sabrina decided not to answer it. Her phone had been ringing continuously all day. She knew it was Tobin. There was nothing he could say to her that would make her feel any different.

As Sabrina exited off the elevator at her job, she saw Tobin outside through the tinted windows. He leaned up against a light pole. Before he could see her, she slipped through a side door to the basement garage. She walked through the garage to another building connected with hers. Sabrina wasn't interested in seeing Tobin - at least not right now.

To get Sabrina out of the house, Trisha took Sabrina shopping. She figured retail therapy was the best course of action. Spending money was always a treat and what best place to wipe any man troubles away but a trip to DSW Designer Shoe Warehouse, Trisha's favorite store.

As Trisha tried on shoes, Sabrina sat in the aisle admiring Trisha's taste in heels. Sabrina wasn't in the mood to shop but got out of the house just to stop listening to the phone ring. Tobin had been calling nonstop and had been sending flowers to her, which she wouldn't accept and had the deliveryman return them or give them away.

"You know Sabrina; men have always been pigs, since the beginning of time," Trisha stated with no care in the world.

"How do you deal with them?"

"You hurt and then you move on to the next one."

Sabrina looked at Trisha with a look of disgust. "Hmmmm, that doesn't sound good."

Trisha grabbed a pair of sandals that were also heels and strapped them up her leg.

"It is what it is. You won't know which type of guy you like until you've tried them all. When mister right comes along, you'll know."

Ain't no way in hell, I'm trying them ALLLLLLL!

Tobin stood across from Blair. The last thing he wanted to do was speak to her, but he was out of options. Sabrina wasn't accepting his calls or his flowers; and Blair was to blame.

"I knew you'd be back. Are you ready to come back home?" Blair said, amused at the fact Tobin had come to visit her.

"Blair we were never together! What the fuck don't you understand about that?"

Blair laughed at Tobin.

"Scandalous ass bitch!" Tobin shouted.

"Is that the best you can do? Really?" Blair walked to the kitchen.

Before Blair could react, Tobin grabbed Blair by her hair from behind and pulled her towards him. He shook her a few times and pushed her to the floor.

"You delusional bitch!" He yelled before spitting on her while she lay on the floor.

The anger inside Tobin continued to swell. He wasn't raised to treat women this way, but to him, Blair wasn't a decent woman. She was hateful, deceitful, and full of trickery. To him, Blair was Satan's sister. After what she did to Sabrina, the lies she told, Blair didn't deserve any respect.

"That's right; call me names, spit on me, if that makes you feel better!" Blair screamed as she wiped his spit from her face and hair.

"Fuck you! Sabrina is what made me feel better!" Tobin yelled.

"It proves you feel something for me. You're here...aren't you?"

Tobin felt like he was having an outer body experience. He had never hit a woman before. His sister was physically abused by her husband, and it took, his brothers, his father, and uncles to set her husband straight. Tobin didn't want to be that man.

Tobin walked to the front door of Blair's apartment. He stood there and stared at the door. He waited for Blair to come after him. If she did, he knew his life would change. There would be nothing stopping him from going to that dark place. Blair was pushing him over the edge.

"Blair, for the sake of everyone, please...please just let me go." Tobin stated calmly.

Tobin paused; he waited for Blair to answer. She didn't. He left.

~

After Tobin left, Blair sat on the floor just where he pushed her. She hadn't moved. Her anger swelled inside of her. She tried to fight back the tears, but they flowed. She crawled over to the television stand and took out her little silver box. She opened it and pulled out a joint. As she smoked it, the scent of the marijuana soothed her. She knew what she had to do. She smoked the entire weed stash she had left and then drank the remaining booze in the two Ciroc bottles she stored for company. Once Blair felt like she was flying, she went into the bathroom. The tears fell down her face as she slammed the door in her face. She then hit herself with anything she could find to make bruises. She messed up the apartment as if there had been a fight; resting on the sofa, she called Sabrina.

Sabrina knocked on Blair's apartment the door. She didn't know what to expect. Blair had called her crying and told her she needed her, would she please come over?

Blair had left the front door slightly cracked; when Sabrina knocked on the door, it slowly opened. Sabrina entered Blair's apartment. She could smell the weed.

"Blair?"

Blair continued to lie on the sofa; she waited for Sabrina to come around down the short hallway.

Blair moaned. "I'm here."

Sabrina stepped up her pace and found Blair hanging halfway off the sofa in the living room.

"Blair! What happened to you?"

Sabrina stumbled over the mess on the floor.

"It was Tobin. He tried to kill me." Blair insisted, in a sweet soft tone.

Sabrina paused. "We need to call the police."

"No... No police," Blair stated.

"Let's get you cleaned up." Sabrina helped Blair to the bathroom.

As Blair washed her face and redid her ponytail, Sabrina fixed Blair some herbal tea she had stashed in her purse. Sabrina handed Blair the tea, and they sat down on the sofa.

"What happened?" Sabrina was curious. Whatever happened between Blair and Tobin; this wasn't the Tobin she knew. She struggled to imagine Tobin being abusive.

Blair gulped for air. "Tobin was here. I guess he was trying to make up..."

Sabrina fought to hold back the tears.

"Well, I don't know what he was trying to do, but he accidentally left this." Blair handed Sabrina a piece of paper with numbers on it. "It must have fallen out of his pocket."

"I think Tobin is HIV Positive." Blair sobbed. "What am I going to do?"

Sabrina read the paper, balled it up and exited to the kitchen as quickly as she could. She needed a moment. What are YOU going to do? Hell, what I am going to do? She thought.

Sabrina and Trisha sat on the floor of Trisha's bedroom. Sabrina cried as Trisha hugged her.

"I can't believe he tried to kill her."

Sabrina didn't want to tell Trisha about Tobin possibly being HIV Positive. She left that detail out.

"I think Blair is deranged if you ask me. You need to talk to Tobin. There are two sides to every story, sis."

Trisha continued to comfort Sabrina.

36

*E*very Sunday evening after the grand Sunday buffet, Cyrus cleaned up the mess the members left. He didn't consider himself a janitor, but he figured it wasn't right to allow his grandfather, Minister Byrd, to pay a cleaning crew a lot of money when he could pay him. Cyrus saw it as a labor of love since Minister Byrd only gave him a third of what a real crew would make.

Cyrus swept the floor and put the tables away when Sabrina entered the basement.

"Hello stranger," she said, in a soft tone.

Cyrus almost dropped the table as he wasn't expecting anyone to be in the church with him. If he waited too late in the evening to clean up, the church had an eerie feeling, like the dead church members were spying on him.

"Whew! You scared me!"

"No, not you." Sabrina half chuckled.

"What brings you here?"

"I need your help."

Cyrus stopped moving the tables to the far wall and

approached Sabrina.

"What's up?"

Sabrina wasn't sure why she was here. She knew what she asked, but didn't know why she would ask Cyrus of all people. Why should he have any faith and trust in me?

"Well, the fact of the matter is, I need your support. I need for you to come with me to the clinic. I need to take a test."

Cyrus paused for a minute. He didn't know what kind of test Sabrina needed to take, but he wanted to know why him.

"Are you pregnant?" He let slip out of his mouth.

Sabrina felt her head pound. This was a mistake.

"No, no, I'm not, but never mind." Sabrina left as quickly as she came.

Sabrina didn't want to get Trisha involved in her situation. Sabrina knew Trisha was a hot head, and if she knew, half the things that were going on, she would have sought Blair, Tobin, Donna and whoever else she could get her hands on, just to beat them into the next lifetime to defend her sister.

Sabrina turned to the only person she could think of that she could trust and wouldn't make a scene about it, Dr. Kent. Sabrina didn't want to meet Dr. Kent at her office. She didn't want the meeting to have a doctor/client feel. She met Dr. Kent at Skate Zone. Sabrina loved to roller skate, and Dr. Kent had never been, but she wanted to ease the tension of everything she felt.

As strange as it may have seemed to Dr. Kent about meeting Sabrina at the roller skating rink, she was always up to trying new things. As they entered the rink, the music came from all different directions. Dr. Kent could feel the vibrations from the bass in her body; the music was loud. Sabrina remembered the days when she would meet her high school friends at the Zone, and they would hang out until it closed. It was a day like this; Sabrina longed for her high school days; no worries or cares.

Dr. Kent skated a short distance on the carpet. The pace on the rink floor was fast; but she only had one option; to get out there and skate. Sabrina watched Dr. Kent go around by herself once. She then went out herself. The movement of the wheels rolling under her feet, and the slight breeze she felt as she turned the corner made her feel free. Free from all her troubles. Sabrina felt like she was floating on air. Yeah!

Once Sabrina went around a few times, and Dr. Kent sat out marveling at Sabrina's grace on skates, Sabrina knew it was time, she confronted the real reason she wanted to speak to Dr. Kent.

"Isn't this great?" Sabrina sat down next to the good doctor.

"If you like skating," Dr. Kent replied, "My feet and ankles are killing me!"

"If you skate often enough, that will fade away."

"You said you needed to see me." Dr. Kent removed her skates and rubbed her feet and ankles.

Sabrina's mind changed from the feeling of freedom to the feeling jailed as she mustered up enough courage to ask Dr. Kent. She already felt rejected by Cyrus, even though she backed out. Cyrus wouldn't have understood, anyway.

Sabrina leaned over close to Dr. Kent's ear. She didn't want the entire skating rink to know her business. "I need your help. I'm in a bad way."

"Are you pregnant?"

"Why does everyone think I'm pregnant?" Sabrina asked. "It's nothing like that. It's something worse."

Sabrina whispered in Dr. Kent's ear. She told her everything. She felt like she was confessing her sins to a priest.

Dr. Kent paused for a moment. Even though, Sabrina didn't meet Tobin at one of her speed dating events, she felt some-what responsible for Sabrina's Blair connection.

"Yes, I'll help you."

Dr. Kent gave Sabrina a tight hug. The strobe lights in the rink continued to dance on the walls.

"However, there is something I should tell you." Dr. Kent mentioned.

Sabrina wasn't sure what Dr. Kent was about to confess, but whatever it was, she looked very concerned.

"I may even be breaking a few patient confidentiality laws, but I think you should know."

"Know what?"

"Your friend, Blair, came to see to me a few times." Dr. Kent took Sabrina by the hand.

"Something isn't right about her. She was talking about trapping her boyfriend, and now I think boyfriend she was talking about was Tobin."

Sabrina looked at Dr. Kent dumfounded, unsure of what to say, Sabrina thanked Dr. Kent, but skated a few more rounds before leaving. She needed to think.

Dr. Kent left the skate rink with one thought on her mind. It was time she paid a visit to Donna.

Dr. Kent entered the Double Sky looking for Donna. She needed to know what was going on with Blair. Dr. Kent called the bar before coming over to ensure Blair was not there. She was in luck it was Blair's day off. She also inquired about Donna. Donna would be in later before the dinner crowd would roll in. Dr. Kent waited.

Dr. Kent's lucky streak continued when Donna came to work before the scheduled time, looking to make extra money with the early shift.

Dr. Kent approached Donna as she put away her things behind

the bar counter.

"May I speak with you in private?" Dr. Kent asked.

"Oh hey, Dr. Kent, what brings you here? Especially, in the middle of the day?" Donna raised her eyebrow.

"I need to have a word with you."

"Ok, let's sit over here." Donna led Dr. Kent to the table near the side of the bar. The Double Sky wasn't busy, so they could speak freely without having to go to the backroom.

"I need for you to tell me more about Blair."

"What do you mean?"

"Like, what is Blair's background? Is she unstable - mentally? Does she do things to harm people?"

Donna wasn't sure where Dr. Kent's line of questioning was coming from. She knew if Blair found out Dr. Kent was at the bar, asking mental health questions about her; she would raise hell.

"I'm not sure if I should answer these types of questions," Donna quipped.

"Well, just tell me what you know."

"Has Blair done something?"

"No. Unless you have something, you want to share."

"All I know is Blair's mother is dead, and her father jetted before she was born. She never had parents; outside of that, I really don't know anything. Blair has her ways, and I don't interfere with that."

Dr. Kent knew she wouldn't get the answers she sought from Donna. A dead end, but at least she could attest to Donna being a loyal friend.

37

*B*lair waited for Charles and Helen to exit the church. She mashed her cigarette on the ground when she saw them leaving. This was her chance to tell them everything going on with Sabrina.

"Mr. and Mrs. Sloan, may I speak to you?"

"No, you may not! We don't want your kind around here." Helen said.

Charles and Helen moved passed Blair and walked to their car.

"It's about Sabrina!" Blair shouted out.

Charles and Helen stopped instantly. Charles hesitated before confronting Blair, "What about Sabrina?" He demanded. He stared into Blair's eyes to look into her soul; instead, he found a familiar face.

Blair stumbled a few steps back. Charles' presence was commanding, something Blair wasn't expecting.

"Sabrina didn't know Tobin, and I were dating, and he's HIV positive." Blair said sobbing.

"Lies!" Helen screamed at Blair. "You are a wicked, wicked

woman. Damn you!" Helen continued with vitriol in her throat as she put her palm in Blair's face. "Blasphemy!"

Blair handed Charles a copy of the doctored test results. He balled the paper up without reading it; and threw it back at Blair.

They left, leaving Blair standing alone with the paper on the ground.

Dr. Kent and Sabrina entered the small-unknown clinic in La Plata. Sabrina found the furthest clinic she could find; somewhere, she knew she wouldn't be seen.

Dr. Kent looked around; the clinic was filled with people who couldn't afford health insurance. With only one seat available, Dr. Kent sat down, but she made sure no one came within an inch of touching her. Sabrina approached the front desk and spoke to the receptionist.

"Take these forms, fill them out, you'll be assigned a number."

While Sabrina took the clipboard from the receptionist, a nurse opened the side door and called out a number.

A man sitting next to Dr. Kent rose as his number was called. He coughed. Dr. Kent covered her face with her suit jacket. Sabrina filled out the forms and returned them to the receptionist.

"Your number is six hundred sixty-six," the receptionist said.

"You're kidding right?" Sabrina asked.

Sabrina shook her head as she sat next to Dr. Kent. Another nurse came from the back.

"Number six hundred and sixty-five," the nurse called out.

"It's going to be okay." Dr. Kent patted Sabrina's leg.

"Number six hundred and sixty-six," the nurse called.

Feeling like she was in a factory for the sick and ill, the way the nurse called out the numbers, Sabrina stood up, and walked to the side door. She paused and then fainted.

When she finally came too, Sabrina was in one of the examination rooms. They had already completed the HIV test, and Dr. Kent was standing over her.

"Let's get you home. It's been a long day."

~

"Now do you believe me?" Helen asked, as she slipped into bed next to Charles.

"We need Minister Byrd." Charles acknowledged.

"We need to set up one of those...inter...thinga ma jiggies," Helen stated.

"An intervention, Helen."

"Yes, one of those."

Charles turned the light off and went to bed.

"Tomorrow, we will speak with Minister Byrd," He admitted to Helen. He realized Sabrina was in a lot of trouble. He didn't think it had gotten this bad.

~

The next day Helen and Charles sat in front of the desk of Minister Byrd. They didn't have an appointment, but Minister Byrd always made time for the Sloans. Minister Byrd still considered them family.

"So, let's go over this again, you all think Sabrina is possessed?" Minister Byrd clarified.

"She's not herself." Charles added.

"This I've seen. I've been taking mental notes myself."

"The devil's got her mind." Helen added.

Minister Byrd paced around his office. "I see."

"We need help. We need to bring Sabrina back into the fold." Helen stated, "We want an inter-convention.

"Helen, It's an INTERVENTION!" Charles let out from frustration.

"Yes, one of those too," Helen said calmly and ignoring Charles' outburst.

"I'll get some of the elders together. Let's knock that devil right outta her!" Minister Byrd reassured the Sloans.

Charles shook the Minister's hand with excitement and joy. He wanted Sabrina to experience life, but now he agreed with Helen. Sabrina's strange behavior had gotten out of control and stranger by the day. She needed God.

"Let us pray," Minister Byrd said.

The three of them bowed their heads in prayer.

38

*C*yrus entered the Double Sky and sat at the bar. He was sure not to speak to Blair or order a drink from her. The last time he was at the Double Sky it was not a pleasant experience.

Blair worked the bar; served drinks looked at her watch; it was time for a break. The other bartender took over, while she stood off to the side and spoke to Donna.

"Love is a trip."

"It's wicked," Donna said.

Cyrus sat closely to where Blair and Donna stood. Blair didn't notice him from Sabrina's church. He leaned over slightly to eavesdrop on their conversation.

"Tobin has been messing around with Sabrina." Blair confirmed to Donna.

"You're joking," Donna said, with minimal surprised. She remembered seeing them at Mookie's.

"Shocker, right?"

"How did you find out?" Donna pressed Blair further. Donna was surprised to see Blair taking the news so well.

"I was going to meet up with Sabrina for a quick dinner, and I saw him standing outside of her office building. I decided to hang back and see what was going on. They kissed and I knew he was the boyfriend she kept mentioning."

"Wow."

"But now they aren't together anymore." Blair snickered.

"What do you mean? What did you do?" Donna wasn't amused.

"I told her he had HIV, and he was the one that did all this." Blair pulled her sleeves up and pointed to her bruises.

Donna gasped and then paused for a moment. "You can be such a bitch sometimes!" Donna walked away.

Cyrus remained glued to his bar stool. He didn't react; he was shocked at what he had learned. Cyrus knew he had to tell Sabrina.

39

*A*fter closing the Double Sky for the night, Blair walked to the Metro. She didn't hear Tobin sneak up on her. He grabbed her, covered her mouth, and pulled her into a small alleyway between the buildings.

"What did you tell Sabrina?" Tobin whispered.

Blair shook her head. He let her go; she almost hit the wall. Tobin looked at Blair and noticed her bruises.

"No wonder Sabrina won't talk to me. You told her I did this to you! Didn't you?"

"Tobin, please!" Blair put her face in her hands and acted as if she was crying.

"Oh, please. My name is Tobin, not Oscar. You aren't academy award-winning material - stop your bitch ass acting. It's not working with me."

Tobin knew Blair was not dealing with a full deck of cards. He didn't want anything more to do with the situation. He had hoped one day he could reconcile with Sabrina, but with Blair around it would never happen.

Tobin disappeared into the night, leaving Blair in the alleyway. Blair let out a sigh.

～

Sabrina checked the messages on her cell phone. She wondered how many times Tobin had called today there were no messages. Instead, she was greeted with a message from Cyrus.

"Cyrus here. It's important you call me. I think I can help you." Sabrina hung up the phone.

"Oh, now you wanna help me?" Sabrina said to the phone and gave it the finger.

～

Dr. Kent sat close to her desk as the buzzer went off; today she had another appointment with Blair. Dr. Kent planned to tell Blair she could no longer accept her as a client.

"Please send her in," Dr. Kent spoke into the phone.

Moments later, Blair walked into the office. She could tell Blair was different. Blair had a sway to her walk. She flopped down on the sofa and gave Dr. Kent a beaming smile.

Then, Dr. Kent glimpsed Blair's bruises. She decided not to ask her about it but waited to hear if Blair offered an explanation first.

"Where are those good candies you usually have?"

"Gone," Dr. Kent said, flatly.

"So, I think I've finally trapped my birdie."

"What have you done?" Dr. Kent said concerned.

"This is confidential right?"

"Always."

Dr. Kent listened to Blair. She put her notepad and pen away in hopes Blair would be more forthcoming. She wanted Blair to feel as comfortable as possible.

Dr. Kent waited patiently for Blair to speak.

Blair snickered, "Wouldn't you like to know?"

Blair changed the conversation. Instead, she spoke of her parents. Especially the father she never knew and how she blamed him for all her mother's problems that led to her death.

Dr. Kent listened to Blair. She concluded Blair dealt with child abandonment issues from both parents. She offered her final diagnosis and release Blair as a client. It was clear to Dr. Kent, Blair wouldn't tell.

Eventually, Dr. Kent tuned Blair out. She wanted to know more about the bruises.

40

*S*abrina walked through the sanctuary. It was dark, and she had no clue why Minister Byrd would summons her to the church at night in the middle of the week.

"Is anyone here?" Sabrina called out as she descended the back staircase.

Sabrina jumped when she saw Minister Byrd appear from the dark shadows. It wasn't like the Minister to be so mysterious.

"Sabrina?" He asked, in his deep booming voice.

"Minister Byrd, you startled me. Is everything okay?"

"I'm so happy to see you here."

Minister Byrd guided Sabrina to a door next to the room where the large Sunday brunch buffets were held. She always wondered what was in that room. Even when she worked at the church, she had never been inside.

"I received your call."

They stopped at the door to the back room, underneath a dim light glowed. Minister Byrd opened the door, as it made a creaking noise.

He needs to get that oiled with the quickness.

Sabrina spotted her parents with a few church elders. The room was illuminated with white burning candles. As Sabrina walked to her parents, Minister Byrd slammed the door shut. He locked it. Sabrina could hear the lock fasten.

"What's this about?" She asked.

There was a long pause. Charles and Helen inched closer to Sabrina; the church elders followed. Minister Byrd remained behind her.

Then the silence was broken.

"Praise God! We are here to save you, child!" Minister Byrd belted out.

Sabrina turned around to look at the Minister with his arms raised high over her head, waving his hands from side to side, with his eyes bulging out.

"What the hell?" Sabrina moved away from the Minister.

Helen clutched her Bible close to her chest, "Lord, save my child!" She cried out.

The other elders hummed hymns in a low tone.

Sabrina looked around the room as Elder Kelly jumped in her face, "Child, you have sinned...but we are here to save you." Elder Kelly preached.

Sabrina turned away from him.

"I don't need to be saved!" Sabrina yelled.

Elder Kelly attempted to place his cold hands on Sabrina's head to pray over her, but Sabrina blocked him with her arm.

"The devil's got her mind!" Charles shouted out.

Sabrina's eyes widened. Never would she have thought her father would take part in an exorcism or whatever they called themselves doing.

Sabrina looked around the room. The room seemed to spin.

'Rebuke Satan, Sabrina! I say rebuke him!" Minister Byrd protested.

Helen rocked back and forth in the chair in the corner. She

waved her Bible in one hand and stomped her foot. "Those wicked people have come and taken my sweet Sabrina from us Lord. We want her back!"

The other church elders continued to hum and provide support to Helen and Charles.

"We are here to help you Sabrina. It's time you come back to the churrrrch!" Minister Byrd preached out in his over booming voice.

"I never left the churrrrch!" Sabrina imitated the Minister.

Sabrina continued to look around the room as everyone prayed.

"We know about your problem," Charles said.

"What problem?"

"You've gotten yourself into a pickle, and we are here to help you," Helen added.

"I'm not in any pickle." Sabrina chuckled at her mother's choice of words.

"Your friend told us you're in trouble," Charles said.

"What friend?"

"That Blair woman," Helen continued.

"She came to us and told us about that HIV positive boy."

"Oh. MY. God." Sabrina paused for a moment. Now she understood why her parents went off the deep end.

"Yes child, he is YOUR God!" Minister Byrd screeched.

"It's going to be okay Sabrina. We're your parents, and we're here to help you." Helen said.

Sabrina had a fire in her eyes. Now she looked possessed.

"Imma kill that bitch!" Sabrina belted as she walked to the door.

Helen passed out. Sabrina jiggled the knob to the door; she turned around and looked at everyone; they were knelling and praying.

"Let me out right now!"

Minister Byrd approached the door. He unlocked it and then stepped in front of the door.

"We are here to knock that devil out of you. But you have to want to be saved, Sabrina."

"If you don't get your old ass from in front of this door; Imma knock something outta you!"

Minister Byrd eyes grew large and moved out of Sabrina's way. She left.

"Possessed is not the word, she's the devil himself!" Minister Byrd screeched, as he watched Sabrina storm out of the room.

41

*B*lair lay across the sofa in a seductive pose as Tobin stood in front of her. She dressed in the sexist Victoria Secret lingerie she owned. He continued to stand over her. Not getting the reaction she wanted, Blair sat up and attempted to touch his face. He deflected her hands away from him.

"You called me. You said it was about Sabrina." He said, in a dry tone.

"I have a proposition." Blair spoke in deep sexy voice.

"First, you can drop that fake ass deep voice; you sound like a man rather than a sexy woman...second whatever it is, the answer is NO!"

Tobin walked to the front door. He knew coming over to Blair's was a mistake. As usual, he didn't get any answers, just more stalking. The only reason he hadn't changed his number was after having it for over five years, many people had it, and he wanted to make sure Sabrina could contact him, just in case she changed her mind.

To stop him, Blair chased him to the door, despite, not having anything worthwhile to say.

"If you don't move back in, I'm going to tell Sabrina two nasty lies. I'll make sure you'll never be with her again!" Blair yelled.

"I knew you were crazy. But what you really are is insane. Don't call me anymore. Rot in hell, you crazy bitch! And I don't give a rat's ass what you tell Sabrina!" Tobin slammed the door in Blair's face.

Despondent from Tobin's words, Blair was left speechless.

Sabrina jogged back to her car from around the lake. She missed Tobin; but jogging was another activity that helped her clear her mind, and she could do it alone. Since the break up, she hadn't gone out. She wanted Tobin, but she wasn't sure if she could trust him again. Sabrina didn't know what to believe.

Sabrina stopped and froze where she stood when she saw Tobin standing there waiting for her. The nerve of him!

"Sabrina!" He called out to her. "I've been looking for you!"

Sabrina wasn't interested in anything Tobin had to say. She wanted to take a dagger and stab him in his chest, right next to his heart, so he could feel the pain and anguish she felt and die a slow death. Tobin approached Sabrina. He didn't want to make her more upset than she already looked. He could sense the anger from her like a heat-seeking missile.

Within inches of her, she turned away from him. Damn he smells good.

The aromas from his cologne made her want to fall into his arms and forgive him for all she had learned, for all she knew Blair could have been lying. Sabrina knew it was possible, given what Dr. Kent told her, but who would bruise themselves to prove a point? Sabrina didn't know Blair that well to say she couldn't have done it, but she could also say she didn't know Tobin that well to say he didn't. It was all complicated and confusing.

"Look at me!"

"Whatever it is you have to say, I don't want to hear it."

Tobin put his face in his hands, wiping the tears away without Sabrina looking.

"I just want to tell you what really happened."

"Oh, you've got to be joking. I saw what REALLY happened."

Ignoring her, Tobin told her everything.

"I was roommates with Blair, yeah we slept together a few times, but that's it," he continued to plead his case. "You've got to believe me Sabrina!"

"That's what you want me to believe, but I've seen what men like you do, you crush women's spirits!" Sabrina shouted back. "Go away Tobin, I don't want to EVER see you again!"

"Is that what you think of me? You know the real me! I was one hundred percent real with you Sabrina!" Tobin pleaded.

Sabrina couldn't take it anymore. She ran to her car and refused to look back. She wanted to believe him, but how could she? Sabrina took a Women's Studies course in college. One topic discussed in the class was about abusive men. Sabrina was clear on the signs to look for, and Tobin was exhibiting all the classics - denial and apologizing.

After Sabrina left, Tobin stood at the park alone. In the near distance, the lake looked peaceful and serene like his life use to be before he met Blair and when he was with Sabrina.

42

As the days rolled into nights and nights back into days, Sabrina's energy continued to fluctuate up and down. One day she could muster enough energy to live her everyday life, other days she couldn't get out of the bed. Today was one of those days. She laid in the bed.

Sabrina hadn't showered; her hair was undone and messy. Clothes were thrown on the floor around her bed, and papers were spread out across her room. She hadn't cleaned her room or her apartment since she, and Tobin broke up. This had been the longest week of her life and the last thing she wanted to do was clean. The messiness fit her mood. Her life was messy.

As Sabrina sat on the bed and looked around at the despair, her phone rang. She looked at the CALLER ID. The screen read: CLINIC, and she answered the phone.

"Hello?" Sabrina paused. "I'll be right there."

She hung up the phone as the weight of the world seemed to crash on her. She rushed to the bathroom, hung her head over the toilet, and vomited. She wanted to know the test results, but she also didn't want to know the results. What would she do if she were

HIV positive? Sabrina knew about HIV and AIDS but had never thought she would ever be placed in a position where she could have contracted the deadly disease. Sabrina always played by the rules, and just when she broke a few, it might cost her, her life.

Patting the sweat off the top of her brow, Sabrina stood at the receptionist desk. She grabbed about seven pieces of tissues from the desk to wipe her hands. The lobby wasn't as crowded as the day she came to take her test. She faced the results alone, instead of dragging Dr. Kent with her.

"I'm here to get my test results," she said, as the pain in her head throbbed harder. Sabrina clutched the edge of the desk. She felt the room spin, all she wanted to do was leave.

The clinic receptionist looked for Sabrina's records in a group of blue file folders piled high next to the computer. Sabrina noticed the folders were stacked so high she could have swiped the first folder and looked at someone's results with ease. That bothered her.

What if someone else knows my results?

"Have a seat, your number one hundred twenty-one will be called shortly," the clinic receptionist said nonchalantly, placing Sabrina's folder on top of the heap.

Before Sabrina could get up enough nerve to ask about their folder confidentially policies, a nurse opened the side door.

"Number one hundred and twenty-one," she called.

That's my number, as she followed the nurse to the doctor's office.

The nurse escorted Sabrina down a long hallway; it seemed to get darker and darker the further she walked. She felt faint. Any moment Sabrina knew she would fall to the floor. She placed her hand on the wall and let it guide her to the doctor's office. As she entered the office, she saw the name Dr. Henry Vasco on the door. She searched for a chair and sat down; she pulled a piece of paper from her purse and fanned herself.

Dr. Vasco had not entered the office, but from the moment, Sabrina sat down, to the moment Dr. Vasco entered the office, it felt like an eternity. He looked at Sabrina fanning herself uncontrollably as he looked at her records before sitting down behind his desk.

"Um, -- ah -- um -- yes...." He tapped his pen on the folder.

Sabrina didn't know what to expect. The room was quiet except for the rhythmic tapping of Dr. Vasco's pen. Sabrina tried to focus and concentrate, but the tapping was all she could hear.

"Yes, what dammit!" She screamed.

"Your test results," he said, with a patient tone. "Let me first tell you that just because..."

Sabrina sighed and snatched the folder from his hands, startling Dr. Vasco.

"I don't have time for all of this! Trust me, I wasn't raised this way, but the tapping and the waiting; I wanted my results, you know what I mean? I'm sorry."

Sabrina read the file, looking for the results.

"Negative!" She lashed out at Dr. Vasco. "That's what I'm talking about!" Sabrina jumped up from her chair and did a little dance, at which time Dr. Vasco snatched the folder back.

"Hey, you don't have to snatch, you know. I was going to give it back!"

Dr. Vasco remained calm. "Well, yes — just because your test result is negative doesn't mean you are not HIV positive."

Sabrina slumped back into the chair.

"Those results say I'm negative. That's the opposite of positive, which means I'm free. I don't have it. Results don't lie!"

"Antibody tests may give false-negative results during the window period," he continued.

"Window period? Does that mean I'm not out of the woods?"

"A window period is an interval of three weeks to six months between the time of an HIV infection and the production of measurable antibodies to HIV. So even though your test shows negative today, it doesn't mean you do not have HIV."

Sabrina slumped further in the chair.

"I want to schedule you for a series of tests."

Sabrina dazed off into the distance. "A series?"

"Yes. Every six months, if nothing has developed in twelve to eighteen months, I'll consider you in the clear. However, my professional medical advice is for you to get regularly tested at least once a year."

Sabrina cried and remained speechless. *What have I done? It isn't Dr. Vasco's problem; I'm in this trouble.*

Sabrina wept.

Sabrina drove through the cemetery, searching for Deacon Byrd's gravesite. She couldn't remember where it was. When they buried him, she never paid attention to the location. She was secretly happy to be free from him, but sadden that death had to be the way out, but that's what the vows said. *I guess he wanted out too.*

After driving around for a minute or two, Sabrina asked one attendant, and he pointed to the section not far from where they were standing. Once there, she prayed over Deacon Byrd's grave.

"I never meant to wish you any harm." She looked down at the gravesite. It was still fresh, and the grass had not grown in. As Sabrina stood over the grave, a warm breeze blew on her.

"I didn't want to marry you but I didn't know how to tell you.

Now I've made a mess of my life. I've met someone. I love him. Please forgive me."

The breeze became stronger the longer she spoke, she thought it was Deacon Byrd. Sabrina stopped speaking as the sun shone brightly on her. She knew at that moment everything would be okay and Deacon Byrd understood. Sabrina left the cemetery comforted. Thank you.

Sabrina paced around her living room while Trisha looked on from an old dining room table Sabrina had picked up from a thrift store.

"When are you going to get living room furniture?" Trisha asked.

"When I feel like it. But that's not of importance at the moment."

Trisha poured ketchup on her fries. "I overheard your parents talking about the exorcism."

"Don't even start me on that hot mess! Those are YOUR parents. I'm claiming adoption. I know they meant well, but it got out of hand!"

"Not before I do. I agree; they meant well; it didn't come out that way. So, what's up? You caught me right in the middle of one of my late-night fast food runs when you called." Trisha bit into her chicken sandwich.

Sabrina exhaled slowly as if was God blowing a sandstorm in the desert. "I got my test results.

"What test results?" Trisha asked, as she approached Sabrina and grabbed her hand.

"I didn't tell you this because I knew you'd go crazy, but Blair told me Tobin was HIV positive, and -"

"And what the hell? Are you serious? I don't believe this trick!

She will stop at nothing! Tobin probably isn't HIV nothing. She said to break you all up. And it worked!" Trisha's voice rose.

"I saw the paper." Sabrina reaffirmed.

"No sis, what you saw was a piece of paper with some phony results."

Trisha felt part of Sabrina's troubles were due to her trying to help her older sister exercise more independence. She didn't expect it to take a sad turn. She meant no harm.

"What did they tell you? Negative, right?"

"Negative. It was negative."

"See, don't even play with me! Imma get this tramp! I swear I am!" Trisha was ready for the fight of the century. She'd do anything to protect Sabrina.

"I have to be tested every six months for about eighteen months before the doctor will clear me."

"What? This is some straight trash! You don't have to do shit but be you and die. I'm telling you this trick is lying!" Trisha hugged Sabrina, regardless of what she said. It could still be a possibility of Blair telling the truth and that Tobin was HIV positive.

"Oh honey...I'm so sorry. I know I'm going off, but I'm here for you."

"You were right," Sabrina said.

Trisha sat down at the table; she looked at her food; she lost her appetite. "About?"

Sabrina sat across from Trisha; she ate two French fries. "I need to find out what happened between Blair and Tobin. There are two sides to every story."

Sabrina and Trisha sat around for moment tapping on the table looking for ideas until the hands of God touched them both equally at the same time.

"DONNA!" They both screamed in unison.

"Blair is off tonight. "Let's go!" Sabrina said.

Sabrina headed for the door; Trisha got her appetite back suddenly, and she grabbed her food.

Sabrina and Trisha stormed into the Double Sky searching for Donna. They had to shift through the crowd; as usual, the bar was packed. Sabrina spotted Donna over in a secluded corner taking an order.

"I see her." Sabrina made her move. Trisha followed.

Once they got to the table, Sabrina and Trisha closed in on Donna; they stood within an inch of her personal space. The couple at the table looked on.

Donna rolled her eyes. "Blair isn't here."

"We're not here for Blair. We want to talk to you."

"Don't you see I'm working?" Donna pointed to the couple. The couple looked back at Donna speechless.

"We're not leaving until you talk to us!" Sabrina demanded.

"You people are fucking up my tips!" She blurted, as she motioned for another server to take over her table. Donna led Sabrina and Trisha to the back room.

Donna escorted Sabrina and Trisha to the backroom of the Double Sky. She sat down a stack of boxes and lit a cigarette. Sabrina stood across from Donna but as far as she could. She hated cigarette smoke. Trisha paced around the room. She wanted to punch Donna in the face, but she knew it wasn't Donna she was mad with; it was Blair. To her, they were the same.

"Why are you all here?" Donna blew smoke out into the air of the small, congested room.

"You know why we're here; you're Blair's best friend. I need to know the truth about her and Tobin," Sabrina demanded. Sabrina inched in closer to Donna.

Damn the smoke!

Donna tried to exit without answering Sabrina. Trisha stepped in front of her blocking her from leaving.

"Where the hell do you think you're going? Sit your ass down!" Trisha shouted.

"Don't be harsh, Trisha."

"I ain't scared of your sister!" Donna shot back.

"We need to get the info! And I'm going to get it out of this heifer; she can believe that!" Trisha punched her fist into the middle of her palm of the opposite hand.

"Like - I - said, I ain't scared of you. I've fought all kinds!" Donna moved in closer to Trisha and made a fist too.

"Sit your ass down!" Trisha pushed Donna into the boxes. "Girl, you don't know me!"

"Both of you sit your asses down! This is a matter of my life, and I want to get information! Lord, please help me!" Sabrina screamed at both Trisha and Donna.

Donna walked to the other side of the room, seeing Sabrina was distressed. Donna didn't have any issues with Sabrina. She didn't like the way they stormed into the Double Sky demanding information as if they were mob girls. They were suburban girls experimenting with the city chicks and had no clue how to play the game. Now they wanted to get tough but getting tough on her job wasn't the place.

"Ok! Blair lied," Donna admitted.

"About what?" Trisha asked.

"About everything! Tobin doesn't have HIV! Tobin has never hit her!" Donna sung like a caged bird.

"I knew that skank was lying!" Trisha punched her hand. She imagined it was Blair's face.

"What else? She's crazy, isn't she?" Sabrina asked, calmly, hoping Trisha would take the hint.

"Blair has a strange way of looking at things. At first, I didn't think she meant any harm, but she was sprung over Tobin like no other man I've seen. She wasn't willing to let him go."

"Did she bruise herself?" Sabrina continued her interrogation.

"YES! Tobin is clean. He loves you Sabrina. Blair is pissed that Tobin left."

Sabrina paced around the room. What do you mean?"

"Blair and Tobin were never together like Blair wanted you to think. They were roommates."

"And?" Trisha asked.

"Look, they got drunk one night, and they had sex. So Blair took it to mean it was more. She kept getting him drunk, so they'd keep having sex. Tobin was never interested in Blair."

"I know a trick when I see one! See Sabrina, my trick senses were up on this one!"

Sabrina sat next to Donna; she placed her had on Donna's shoulder. "Thank you."

Donna admired Sabrina and wished she could be more like her. "No problem. I'm sorry, sorry I didn't come forward sooner. Things happen." Donna felt remorseful about what happened to Sabrina, but she wanted slap the shit out of Trisha.

Sabrina left the back room, but Trisha lingered for a moment. She wanted to say something extra to Donna, but the pitiful look on her face was more than enough satisfaction.

Sabrina and Trisha stood in front of the Double Sky.

"I told you that hooka was no good!" Trisha belted out.

"I know, but now we have work to do!"

It was pay back time.

~

Tobin took small sips of his beer as he lounged in an old Lazy Boy chair Mike had on his back porch. Mike flipped burgers on the grill in the backyard while Tobin looked on. Mike's kids played in the blow up baby pool next to the picnic table. Mike's wife continued to move between the kitchen and backyard, just when the heel of her shoe got stuck in the grass.

"MIKKKKKKE!" She yelled in horror.

"Honey...I told you not to wear those things in the grass!" Mike yelled back while keeping an eye on the food.

Tobin continued to sit in the lounge chair, limp and slumped over. He turned away from Mike and his family as a tear fell from his face. His world was ending; Sabrina was gone. He would never be with her again.

43

*S*itting in one pew in the back of the church Sabrina thought back in time. She thought about her wedding, the day she brought Blair to the church, then turned around and brought Tobin. She even thought about the night of the intervention fiasco. So much has happened with her and the church; Sabrina didn't want any drama from her parents or the church elders and members. Her head hung low while her shoulders drooped.

Sabrina could see her father from her seat, but she didn't see her mother. It was unlike Helen not to show up for church. Sabrina could understand why her mother wouldn't want to come. The intervention didn't go as planned and Sabrina said a few choice words she normally wouldn't have shouted in the house of the Lord or anywhere. The choir sang as more members came in. Minister Byrd stood at the pulpit and spotted Sabrina in the back in her dark sunglasses.

"Let us turn to the wisdom of the book of Job!" Minister Byrd yelled and then pointed to the congregation. "We have friends who whitewash their advice with lies! God cannot be deceived! And the misfortunes of evil deeds. We suffer at our own doing. God doesn't make us suffer," he yelled as loud as he could, "Reach out to God to heal your suffering! Let the church as AMEN!"

"AMEN!" The congregation let out in unison; with a few members turning around to give Sabrina the evil eye.

Sabrina wasn't surprised at the looks or the sermon, but she stayed.

"I deserve this," she thought.

Sabrina was the last person to make her way down to the basement to get a plate of food. Before she could get down the stairs, Minister Byrd grabbed her arm and stopped her. He kindly smiled at Sabrina and pulled her to the side. He didn't want any of the church members seeing him speaking to her, and he didn't want her to pull another stunt like she did at the intervention.

"You're no longer welcome here," he said.

"What?"

"Please leave."

I've really become a bad person if Minister Byrd wants me to leave.

Sabrina never thought Minister Byrd would ask a church member to leave. She believed in her heart he was a forgiving man, but perhaps this was the right thing to do.

She didn't want to make a scene; the church probably already knew about the intervention and how she acted out. She left quietly. As she walked by the entrance to the basement, she saw her father sitting at the table alone. His eyes were sad. She hadn't spoken to her parents since they tried to exorcise her demons, but she was at a loss for words. She knew they didn't mean any harm, but her problems were not theirs to fix. Her problems were her problems and not the devil as Helen had claimed. Helen told everyone in the church Sabrina was possessed.

Sabrina walked to her car, disappointed; she felt like she didn't have anywhere to go. As Sabrina unlocked her car door, Cyrus ran to her.

"Sabrina!" Cyrus called to her.

"What is it Cyrus? Did you know Minister Byrd would kick me out the church?

"No I didn't. Did you get my message?"

"I saw that you called."

"You didn't call me back."

"No. I didn't. What do you want?"

Sabrina wasn't appreciating Cyrus' long-windedness. She wanted to go home and cry all her sorrows away. He was holding her up from being depressed and having an excuse to eat every sweet known to man.

"I know your friend Blair set Tobin up."

"How do you know?"

"I went to the Double Sky one night, and I overheard her talking to someone about what she did."

Sabrina stood by her car and listened to Cyrus. She wondered why he didn't tell his family she was set up by Blair.

"Well, why didn't you tell your family Blair was spreading these lies about me? You knew all this time and didn't say anything!"

Sabrina contained her anger. She knew it wouldn't help her situation getting upset with Cyrus, but she thought he could have done more to help.

"I called you, but you didn't call me back."

"True." Sabrina knew Cyrus was right.

"I figured I'd tell you first, and you could do what you wanted with the information. It wasn't my place to tell my family anything. They are your family too, believe it or not."

Sabrina realized how mean she had been to Cyrus over the years. She knew he had a crush on her, and she treated him like a second-class citizen, when he always was friendly.

"It's okay Cyrus. Thanks for the info."

"Now, go get the bitch!"

Did Cyrus just curse?

Sabrina laughed at Cyrus. That statement alone helped Sabrina feel better. She felt empowered. She would get the bitch!

Sabrina gave Cyrus a kiss on the cheek, then got in her car and drove away. It was time she took the situation back into her hands. No longer feeling sorry for herself, Sabrina wanted to make Blair pay for all her sins.

Sabrina waited in Dr. Kent's office. She was sure not to touch anything. She wasn't certain if Dr. Kent had forgiven her, so she stood in the middle of the office with her hands crossed. This way, she wouldn't be charged with touching anything.

As Sabrina stood in the middle of the floor trying to look inconspicuous, Dr. Kent rushed into the office.

"You're here, great. Let's take a walk."

It was a beautiful day in Washington, DC. There were no clouds in the sky, the sun shone, and the temperature was warm but not too warm. It was the perfect day to take a walk. Dr. Kent thought it would be nice for her and Sabrina to get out of the office. It wasn't as if Sabrina was a formal patient. Dr. Kent never charged Sabrina for her services, so why not do something informal and spontaneous.

Dr. Kent's office was not far from the Washington DC zoo; they hopped on the red line Metro train and made their way up Connecticut Avenue. Dr. Kent thought it would be nice to check out the panda exhibit.

"Isn't it a wonderful day?" Dr. Kent bought cotton candy from the vendor.

"It's lovely. Well, the reason I wanted to speak to you was because I got my test results back."

"And?"

Sabrina and Dr. Kent walked pass the lion house.

"Negative, the test came back negative, but my doctor wants me to come in every six months to be tested for the next eighteen months."

Dr. Kent went into her psychology bag. "How does that make you feel?"

Dr. Kent wanted to get a sense of Sabrina's state of mind. In working with a few of my patients who have had the same kinds of scares, they either become very withdrawn from life, or they become even more reckless, thinking they are invincible. Dr. Kent wasn't sure which side Sabrina was leaning toward.

"Sad. I allowed myself to be placed in this situation, even at my doing."

Dr. Kent felt Sabrina's statement was a positive move in the right direction; that she was grieving and understanding her situation fully.

"But that's not even the half of it. I mean I went through all this turmoil, and then I find out that Blair lied about it all. Tobin isn't and never was HIV positive. He was Blair's roommate, nothing more - but they slept together a few times when she got him drunk."

Sabrina felt a sense of relief when she told Dr. Kent the truth.

"Oh Sabrina." Dr. Kent knew Blair was up to something wicked, but she couldn't put her finger on it.

"Tobin was telling me the truth. I feel bad because I didn't recognize when the man I love needed me to believe in him. I couldn't do it."

"Don't blame yourself. You didn't know, but now you do, and it's all within your power to fix it."

The words Dr. Kent spoke were comforting to Sabrina. It was within her power to fix everything.

"It's no different from being caged like those lions; I suppose," Sabrina said, as she looked at the lions walking around their limited space. "I once felt caged, I know how that feels."

"Always choose your friends wisely," Dr. Kent interjected.

"You can say that again."

"Always choose your friends wisely."

They both laughed as Dr. Kent offered Sabrina some cotton candy.

44

$\mathcal{B}$ored in the house, Donna and Blair went to hang out; they decided on bowling. It was a nice drive down route 50 to Crofton. Somehow, Donna convinced Blair there were always good-looking men at the bowling alley, but tonight it was a little thin; it was after ten at night, and the leagues were done.

Donna looked for a ball while Blair followed; they went back and forth up and down the lanes looking for a ball. As they approached their lanes, Donna said, "Sabrina and her sister came pass the Double Sky."

"What are you talking about?" Blair put her ball on the rack and changed her shoes.

"I had no choice, Blair. I told them the truth."

She stood in front of Donna and raised her eyebrow. "What truth? The truth about what?"

"Oh, come on, this shit needs to stop! You know exactly what I'm talking about." Donna paused. "I'm talking about your lies and your little schemes to get back at Tobin for being with Sabrina."

The rage bubbled through Blair's veins the more Donna spoke;

she tried to maintain her composure, but before she knew it, she slapped Donna across her face.

"You had no fucking right to tell them shit. That's my business." Blair stood over Donna. "Fuck! Now what am I going to do?" Blair mumbled to herself.

Donna grabbed the side of her face. She blinked a few times before she realized she was slapped. She sat in her seat stunned.

"Oh, no the fuck you didn't!" Donna's eyes widened and lunged at Blair.

As they hit the floor, Donna clawed at Blair's face.

"You want bruises bitch? Imma give you some real bona fide bruises!" Donna belted.

Blair squirmed on the floor clutching Donna's hair. The crowd at the end of the bowling alley ran to Blair and Donna fighting to catch all the commotion as the women fought on the floor.

"Fuck you!" Blair screamed, while pulling a patch of Donna's hair out.

"Video it!" One of young people in the crowd called out.

Most of the people in the crowd caught the moment on video and uploaded it to YouTube just when the Anne Arundel County police jumped in to stop the fight.

"Show's over!" The police shouted.

Donna and Blair were escorted out of the bowling alley and placed into two different squad cars.

Sabrina knew now was the time strike against Blair. She was worn out and tired of dealing with the endless lies and rumors swirling around the church. She knew it was time to put this to rest if not for the sake of herself but for her mother. Trisha told Sabrina how Helen had stopped going to church after the intervention. She was too embarrassed to face anyone.

Sabrina missed Tobin. She had to figure out a way to make things right with him.

Sabrina grabbed her phone and called Blair. "Blair this is Sabrina...meet me at the church on Sunday. I'd like to talk to you."

Sabrina hung up the phone comforted that Blair didn't pick up.

She then called Donna. Donna didn't answer either. Sabrina wanted Donna at the church to verify her story.

45

Trisha decided Sabrina needed a change of pace. She had been moping around since she and Tobin broke up. In the last few months, she got married, watched her new husband passed away, quit her job, changed her appearance, met a wonderful man - who could be HIV positive, and encountered the craziest woman she'd ever met in her life. Given the circumstances, Trisha knew the best thing for Sabrina was to take her out on a date and show her how to get her life back on track.

Trisha and Sabrina walked into Mookie's Jazz Club. The music was soothing to Sabrina's soul. She swayed her head to the tunes of the jazz band.

Trisha knew she shouldn't have taken Sabrina back to Mookie's, but she figured life goes on, and she couldn't allow this madness to stop Sabrina from going to places she enjoyed.

"I haven't been here since...since...well, you know," Sabrina said.

"Time to let Tobin go. Put him behind you."

As they moved to their reserved table, the man at the bar gave Trisha a nod. She nodded back, and he walked towards them.

"Don't get yourself all flustered over one guy; there are too many fish in the sea," Trisha said, as the tall, mocha skinned man approached them.

"Care to dance?" He asked Sabrina.

"No, no thank you," Sabrina said politely. The man reminded her of Tobin.

"Why not?" Trisha asked, "It's just a dance Sabrina, not a marriage proposal." Trisha smiled at her.

Sabrina paused for a moment. She knew Trisha was right. There was no sense in her not enjoying the night.

"Okay, why not!" she took his hand guiding her to the dance floor.

After Trisha dropped Sabrina off at her apartment, Sabrina felt alone. She went to the bathroom and stared into the mirror. There was a look of sadness in her eyes; small bags formed from the excessive crying. With no makeup on, Sabrina's face appeared worn out, from all the stress, she noticed splotches on her cheeks. The M*A*C studio fix did a good job covering up most signs of her tired worn-out face.

As she continued to stare at herself in the mirror, she screamed at herself as she banged her fist on the mirror. A slight crack appeared and blood ran down her hand.

Sabrina cried, "Everything is just a mess!"

46

The Double Sky opened before midday for customers to have lunch. There was a light crowd already forming. Donna looked at her watch and then stepped outside. She paced in front of the bar and took out a cigarette from her bra. She sat outside in the warm air and took long drags. She soon noticed Tobin walking towards her.

"I'm glad you could come," Donna said.

"What do you want Donna? I'm not trying to run into Blair."

"Blair doesn't work here anymore. She quit."

"Figured as much, but seriously, you called me down here to tell me that? You could've saved that for the phone," Tobin huffed.

"Well, see...Blair and I...well we got into a huge fight."

"And what does that have to do with me?"

"You could probably YouTube it." Donna laughed.

"Again, why are you telling me this? I don't care," Tobin restated.

"Blair told Sabrina a pack of lies and I didn't say anything. I knew she had fibbed about the HIV test results...and the..."

"The what? What HIV?"

"Blair told Sabrina that she thought you were HIV-positive and she showed Sabrina a doctored test result. She also bruised herself to make it look like you tried to kill her."

"That muthafuckin bitch! I knew she was crazy!"

"I'm so sorry; I should have told you sooner." Donna empathized with Tobin's pain and anger.

Donna tried to calm Tobin down as he cursed and ranted about Blair.

"Thanks Donna, I need to go find Sabrina." Tobin hugged Donna and walked away from the bar. But before Tobin could get a good distance away, Blair pulled up. Donna and Tobin stare as she exited her car.

"Well, well, well...what do we have here?" Blair suspected Donna and Tobin standing together.

Tobin lunged for Blair's throat. He wrapped his hands around her neck, mumbling a string of obscenities as Blair tried to break free. Donna pulled at Tobin, but he didn't let go. Donna yelled for help. One of the assistant managers ran out of the bar and separated Tobin from Blair.

Blair coughed and held her neck.

"SHE ISN'T WORTH IT!" Donna shouted.

"Oh, shut up! Fuck you and yeah fuck you too!" Blair shouted back.

"You don't deserve shit with your spiteful ass!" Donna yelled at Blair.

Donna left. She knew if she didn't, she and Blair would fight again.

Tobin followed Donna. "Did you set this up?"

"I swear I didn't," she said.

Crossing her fingers, Donna hoped when Tobin saw Blair, he'd punch her in the face, but choking her out was just as good.

47

_L_ike any other Sunday morning, Charles drank his coffee at the kitchen table, while Helen called herself cooking breakfast and as usual, the frying pan burned.

Charles waved his hands back and forth from the smoke. The smoke alarm went off and Helen swatted the dishtowel to clear the smoke.

Sabrina entered from the back porch into the thick smoky aired kitchen.

"Sabrina? Is that you?" Helen asked.

"Sweet Lord!" Sabrina let out; kissing her father on what she thought was his forehead but was his bald patch. "I'm so sorry," as she patted his head.

"Listen...I have something I want to say."

Trisha entered the kitchen.

"I know I've been rude. I've hurt you. I've done things you're not proud of...but I needed adventure. That's no excuse. But I'm asking for your forgiveness. I apologize for my behavior."

"Sabrina...we understand...so much has happened to you in last few months..." Helen interjected.

"I love you guys. You all are my family, and I don't know what I'd do without you," Sabrina continued.

Sabrina needed to let her family know how much, they meant to her. They were the only family she had. Regardless, if her father never spoke over ten words in the mornings, or if her mother couldn't cook and even Trisha was worldlier than she was. She needed their love and support. She was proud to be a Sloan. And she wanted them to know she cared about them.

"It's always about family. My family." Sabrina added.

"Family hug!" Trisha shouted.

The family hugged.

Trisha glanced over to look at the burnt food. "Oh ma...you've been trying to cook again! That's it! I'm getting you cooking lessons."

The family laughed.

Sabrina grabbed her things. "I have to get to the church before you all come, but I hope to see you there - especially you ma."

Helen smiled.

Sabrina left out the back door.

48

*B*efore church started, Sabrina wanted to explain her side of the story regarding all the rumors that infiltrated the church. She stood in the pulpit next to Minister Byrd. The church parishioners whispered while others weren't as shy and shouted at the minister for allowing Sabrina to stand next to him. This reminded Sabrina of the union meetings she would attend with her father when she was younger. The crowd was always feisty.

"Now, now, family let us calm down. Sabrina will talk," Minister Byrd said, with a soothing voice and handed her the microphone.

Sabrina spoke with Minister Byrd between his early morning and regular church services. She asked for his forgiveness after she apologized for her rude behavior. She confided in him everything that happened, and he was more than willing to forgive Sabrina and welcomed her back into the church.

Just as Sabrina was about to speak, Charles and Helen walked into the sanctuary. Sabrina glimpsed her parents walking down the aisle and pushed forward with her speech.

"I know you've heard things about me. Some things that could be true, but a lot of them are not."

Just at the moment, one of the older church members jumped up and waved his collapsible cane in the air.

"We heard you're a harlot, and you've got that nasty person's disease!" He ranted, as his cane almost hit him.

Just then, another older woman stood up. "I heard them young people call it the package. It's delivered and you deliver it to others," she said, with an awful frown.

Sabrina paused for a moment. She knew the members of the church were furious. Helen was one of the most important women in the church, and Sabrina embarrassed her, and disrespected the Christian principles her mother taught her. Sabrina knew there were things expected of her, and everyone understood it was Trisha that was more likely to be in this kind of situation.

"How you gone bring the devil all up in the Lord's house?" Elder Kelly shouted.

"Let Sabrina speak!" Charles intervened.

Sabrina mouthed to her father, "Thank you."

"I was tested and I'm negative. I never had HIV, or AIDS or any sexually transmitted disease."

"Oh no she didn't put her sexual business out in the street," one of the younger members of the church said.

"And you can't get rid of it!" The older woman shouted again.

"The girl who I thought was my friend...well she wasn't," Sabrina continued, "And I know she was the one that was telling everyone the lies about me."

Before Sabrina could speak another word, Blair entered the church. The door slammed. Everyone turned to see who it was.

"That's her!" Sabrina pointed to Blair. "She lied about everything!"

"LIES! You stole my boyfriend, you lying bitch!" Blair slurred.

Sabrina stepped down from the pulpit, "Tobin was never your boyfriend!"

Sabrina could feel the blood rushing from all parts of her body to her head. It pounded. The anger she felt inside was coming to boil. Sabrina walked to Blair.

Sabrina and Blair stood eye to eye, with fists curling into balls, and then Donna ran into the church.

"And who are you?" Minister Byrd asked.

"I'm the liar's ex-best friend. She attacked me at the bowling alley when I let her know, I told Sabrina and Trisha about her lies!"

"Well, speak on child, what's going on?" Minister Byrd continued.

"Blair set up Tobin because he rejected her. They were only roommates!"

"You lying ass bitch! I don't need this shit from any of you old fake ass holier than thou, pork eating, wino muthafuckas!" Blair screamed.

"EWWWWW!" The church members said in unison.

That's when Sabrina had had enough of Blair's antics, and she shoved Blair towards the floor, as she fell, Blair tried to grab Donna.

"Get the hell off of me!" Donna screeched.

Donna pushed Blair, and Blair went toward Sabrina and at the same moment, Sabrina lunged for her. The two women rolled and tussled on the floor until Sabrina could get the upper hand.

Minister Byrd tried to grab Blair from Sabrina, but Blair punched Minister Byrd. Minister Byrd fell to the ground as Cyrus pulled Sabrina off Blair.

"STOOOP! This IS the house of the Lord, people!" Cyrus yelled.

Blair stumbled as she tried to stand, with her eye swelling; she spat blood on the floor.

Sabrina tried to hold back the tears, but the emotions of what she had been through came to the forefront.

"You tried to hurt me. You tried to hurt my family. I'm going to get him back!"

Charles grabbed Sabrina as the tears rolled down her face.

"That's enough Sabrina. She gets the point," Charles said, just as Trisha ran into the church.

Trisha looked around. Blair slumped over on the pews, and Charles held Sabrina close.

"Why do I always miss the good fights?" Trisha said, as she stomped her foot.

Blair stood up and walked right to Sabrina's face. She looked Sabrina in her eyes. From her back pocket, she pulled out the picture of her parents. On the back, it read C.S. and me. For a long-time, Blair couldn't figure out the faded initial, but then she realized it was for Charles - Charles Sloan. Blair knew she had seen Charles before, she couldn't remember where.

Blair pushed the faded picture into Sabrina's face.

"Charles Sloan is my father!" Blair let the entire church know. The tears streamed down her face.

Everyone in the church gasped in unison.

Charles snatched the picture from Blair. "This isn't true." Until he studied the faded photo; then it came back to him.

Charles sat down in the pew and wept.

"Daddy, tell these people that's not true!" Trisha begged.

Charles had fallen in love with Blair's mother, Isabella, when she was only nineteen years old. She was the niece to a well-known underboss of a mob family - a white mob family. Charles was black, and it wasn't acceptable for her to date a black man. He was from Bedford-Stuyvesant and she was from Bensonhurst. Their love was forbidden.

"I didn't know Isabella was pregnant. One day she disappeared, and I never saw her again." Charles admitted.

"Well, she came to live in Washington, DC; she got on drugs, became a prostitute, and then she died!" Blair cried. "She left New York City, and she was never the same and you never came for her!"

"Word on the street was that the associates and soldiers were looking for me, so I left. And I ended up in a small town in Virginia. I met Helen, and my life changed. I never knew she bore a daughter."

"Charles!" Helen was in disbelief, she never knew why Charles came to Virginia, only that he was looking for decent work.

Sabrina and Trisha held their breath waiting for Charles to explain more.

Charles paused and sighed. "Yes, it could be true."

Helen screamed in an outrage. Everything she had worked for in her marriage. The man she thought Charles was; he wasn't.

"Helen, I don't love you any less. I didn't know." Charles acknowledged.

What the hell are we going to do now?

"Well ain't this some shit. She ain't my sister!" Trisha miffed.

Everyone stood in silence. Sabrina felt ill. She whipped her older sister's ass over a man. Trisha was also confused and stood in doubt. And Helen couldn't speak or look Charles in the eye. She felt betrayed.

"We all need to pray." Minister Byrd said. "Forgiveness is needed, but I'm going to ask Blair to leave. We won't solve these problems all in one day." Minister Byrd was calm. "I will ask Blair to come back another day to work it out."

Cyrus grabbed Blair by the arm and dragged her to the door.

"This ain't over!" Blair screamed before leaving.

"Stick a fork in her...she's done!" Cyrus hollered.

Trisha rolled her eyes at Cyrus. "Could you have been just a bit cornier?

Helen approached Sabrina, "I'm so sorry, mom." Helen hugged Sabrina with all the strength she had.

Trisha joined the hug, then Minister Byrd and Cyrus joined, even Donna inched over and joined in.

Cyrus grabbed Donna by her waist.

"Oooh," Donna said.

"Yeah baby," Cyrus replied.

Charles wanted to join in, but the look Helen gave him was cold blooded. He stood back and allowed Helen to have her moment with Sabrina and Trisha.

Helen noticed Charles standing off to the side by himself. She loved her husband. He didn't know, she reasoned. Helen was a real Christian woman; forgiveness was in her heart. She inched over to Charles.

"I forgive you," she whispered.

Charles grabbed Helen and held her close. "I'm sorry." He whispered back.

The church cheered more.

Everyone in the church gave one another a hug.

49

Tobin found a parking space near Sabrina's apartment building. He grabbed the dozen of red roses from the back seat. He had about half a block to walk. He went over in his mind what he wanted to say, how he wanted to say it, and how he wanted to grab and kiss her. He wasn't sure how Sabrina would react to him, showing up to her place without calling. Donna had filled him in on the fight at the church between Sabrina and Blair; and how they were half-sisters.

He tried calling Sabrina a few times. She didn't answer, and he didn't leave a message. He wanted to make everything right between them in person.

Once Tobin reached the front of the building, he stopped. He felt heaviness in his chest. It was a feeling he had never had before. He paced along the sidewalk, working up a sweat, almost damaging the roses as his arm swung up and down while he talked to himself. He knew any minute Sabrina would leave to go to work, and he thought this was a good time as any to explain everything and show her how much he loved her.

As he paced back and forth, Ralph, Sabrina's older silver-haired door attendant, watched him.

"She's still home you know." Ralph grinned.

Ralph noticed the distress in Tobin's eyes and wanted to help him out. He knew something was wrong between Sabrina and Tobin when he didn't see the fellow come around anymore and how Sabrina's pretty face looked sad every day. He figured they had broken up, but he thought they were a nice-looking couple.

Tobin made a dash for the door then stopped. "Am I making a mistake?" He asked Ralph.

"Good love is never a mistake, son. Sometimes, you gotta make a fool of yourself and be happy!" Ralph exclaimed.

Feeling empowered Tobin rushed into the building and to the elevator. He continued to press the up button. It didn't make the elevator come any faster. He walked around in a circle, continuing to look at the display to see which floor the elevator was on. He ditched the elevator and take the stairs.

Sabrina stood in the hallway and waited for the elevator. When the elevator arrived, she got on. The doors closed.

Tobin ran from the stairway passed the closing elevator doors and down the hall. He banged on Sabrina's door.

Sabrina exited the elevator. She stopped for a moment in the front lobby in front of the mail slots. She searched her purse for her keys.

∾

Tobin stood at Sabrina's door. He looked at the bouquet of roses; they were looking like they took a beat down; a mirrored emotion to how he was feeling. He knocked one more time. There was no answer. He realized he must have missed her by taking the stairs. Tobin ran back down the hall to the stairway; waiting for the elevator would take too long.

∾

Sabrina stopped outside the front of her building and flipped through her mail. She tilted her head back and let the sun shine on her face. The warmth of the sun comforted her. As she stood there, Ralph approached her.

"Hold that thought, I forgot my keys. Sorry Ralph, I'll be right back."

Sabrina left Ralph standing there while she went back to the lobby to get her keys, still hanging from the mail slot. She grabbed them and exited.

Sabrina went back over to Ralph.

"Good Morning, Ralph!" Giving him a wave.

Ralph tipped his hat to Sabrina and paused for a second. "I think you should wait here Miss Sabrina."

Sabrina raised her eyebrow. "Why? I wanted to get to Starbucks before getting to work, and you know the Starbucks on 20th Street is always busy."

Sabrina looked at her watch.

"Yes, I do understand. But you know love is patient."

Sabrina didn't quite understand Ralph's comment. "Okay," was all she could say as she left Ralph.

∾

Tobin ran into the lobby, sweat dripped from his forehead. The once full looking bouquet of long stem red roses was now looking like a bunch of weeds, he picked up along with the way. Tobin looked franticly for Sabrina in the lobby before dashing out to the street.

"She went towards the corner." Ralph pointed.

Sabrina walked to the corner of the street. Tobin saw Sabrina from a distance. She waited and dropped her keys while fumbling through her purse and holding her mail. As she stooped down to pick up the keys; Tobin grabbed her hand. Sabrina snatched her hand away from him. As they stood face to face, he pulled her in closer.

"Hey," he said.

At the sight of him, a tear fell from Sabrina's face.

"I'm sorry," she said.

Tobin kissed her before she could pull away. Sabrina touched his cheek.

"Slow. Let's go slow."

"Yeah, slow - so do you have time for coffee before work?"

"A venti caramel macchiato?" Sabrina asked.

Sabrina took a step back, gave Tobin a wide smile and then tossed her keys in the air. He looked at them as they fell from the powder blue sky and caught them.

"Yeah, a venti caramel macchiato."

They walked down the street - together - hand in hand.

In the distance, Blair, wore dark shades to cover her black eye. She leaned against the light pole, lit a cigarette, and let it hang from her busted lip. She stared at Sabrina and Tobin as they walked down the street together. And of course...she followed them.

The drama continues...

ALSO BY MICHELLE CAREY

Blair X (part two to Church Chick)

Twisted (part three to Church Chick

Let It Burn

Jinxed

www.ingramcontent.com/pod-product-compliance
Lightning Source LLC
Chambersburg PA
CBHW032155190626
46808CB00020B/460